Towers of Light

ALLEN BROKKEN

CONTENTS

1. Introduction
2. Teacher Guide
3. LIGHT OF MINE UNIT STUDY
4. STILL SMALL VOICE UNIT STUDY
5. FEAR NO EVIL UNIT STUDY
6. ARMOR OF GOD UNIT STUDY
7. WELLSPRING OF LIFE UNIT STUDY
8. DEMOLISHING THE STRONGHOLD UNIT STUDY
9. Answer Key

ALLEN BROKKEN

Allen Brokken is a teacher at heart, a husband and father most of all. He's a joyful writer by the abundant grace of God. He began writing the Towers of Light series for his own children to help him illustrate the deep truths of the Bible in an engaging and age-appropriate way. He's dedicated fifteen years of his life to volunteer roles in children's ministry and youth development.

Now that his own children are off to college, he's sharing his life experiences on social media @allenbrokkenauthor and through his blog https://allenbrokkenauthor.com/blog.

INTRODUCTION

Dear Reader,

When my children were middle-grade readers, I had a tough time finding adventure stories they could enjoy that also emphasized Biblical truths. So I began telling them a story about life on the frontier, weaving in points of the faith that I felt they should learn. As the story developed, a unique world of pets with fantastic powers and holy weapons emerged to help the young characters hold back the forces of darkness.

The *Towers of Light: Complete Series of Unit Studies for Homeschoolers* is a supplement to those tales of adventure. It digs deeper into the spiritual aspects of the story from a Christian perspective. Over the next four weeks, your students will study passages from the story to highlight lessons from scripture and their real life application. There are also activity pages and memory verses to help them internalize the key messages in the Towers of Light.

I hope you enjoy the story as much as my own children did.

May God bless you richly,

Allen Brokken

ACTIVITIES MATERIALS LIST

1. Aluminum foil
2. Balloons
3. Baking soda
4. Ball-point pen, markers, & pencils
5. Blue and red cellophane (clear, colored plastic binder dividers will work)
6. Borax
7. Box cutter (for adults) & scissors
8. Cardboard shoebox & cardboard pieces in assorted sizes
9. Card stock
10. Cereal box
11. Clothing iron
12. Coffee
13. Construction paper—white & colored
14. Craft jewels—small, assorted
15. Dirty pennies
16. Disposable gloves
17. Distilled water
18. Egg
19. Empty milk jug
20. Food coloring
21. Glass bowl—small
22. Glass fish tank or bowl
23. Glass jars—at least one lid with a rubber seal
24. Glitter
25. Glycerin or baby oil
26. Gravel or pebbles—small
27. Hot glue & school glue
28. Index card
29. Lemon juice
30. Model Magic clay
31. Old broomstick or mop handle
32. Orange (fruit)
33. Paint—tempura & acrylic
34. Paint brushes

1. Paper cups
2. Paper plate
3. Paper towels
4. Pipe cleaners
5. Plants—small
6. Plastic container with lid—small, shallow, & square
7. Plastic figurines—small, assorted, waterproof
8. Plastic grocery bag
9. Plastic water bottle with cap (empty)
10. Plastic wrap
11. Playdough
12. Pool noodle
13. Popsicle sticks
14. Potting soil
15. Q-tip
16. Rubber bands
17. Ruler & tape measure
18. Saline solution
19. Salt
20. Seeds—bird feed & plants
21. Shoes—adult boots, adult flip-flops, & youth athletic shoes
22. Spoon
23. Straws
24. String & yarn
25. Sugar cubes
26. Tape—scotch & duct
27. Timer
28. Tissue paper—white & colored
29. Toliet paper tube
30. Toothpick
31. Tweezers
32. Wax paper
33. White vinegar
34. Wood dowel rods

TEACHER GUIDE

EDUCATIONAL GOALS

The *Towers of Light: Complete Series of Unit Studies* was developed for the Towers of Light book series, a Christian fantasy adventure for middle-grade readers. It combines Biblical values and educational activities in four weeks of supplemental curriculum.

Story passages, chapter assignments, activities, and thoughtful questions foster Biblical discussion while exercising reading comprehension and critical thinking skills. Vocabulary exercises and puzzles expand students' vocabulary and provide an opportunity for students to use their references skills while also exercising their critical thinking skills. Memory verse copy work helps students learn scripture as they practice their handwriting, and coloring sheets offer a fun opportunity for creative expression.

SUGGESTED PACING

Each unit study in the series is designed to be completed within four weeks. Each week includes fifty to sixty pages of content, which can be read aloud or independently. Students are encouraged to keep a reading journal for their memory verse copy work, vocabulary exercises, and to record their answers to the reading questions.

DAYS ONE THROUGH FOUR

- In their reading journal, have students copy the MEMORY VERSE and complete the VOCABULARY EXERCISE.
- Read the STORY PASSAGE aloud and discuss the passage question as a group.
- Complete the DAILY READING assignment, aloud or independently.
- After reading, students should record their answers to the READING QUESTIONS in their journal. Answers may also be discussed as a group.

DAY FIVE

- Complete the DAILY READING assignment, aloud or independently.
- Have students recite the MEMORY VERSE.
- Use the COLORING PAGE, PUZZLE, and ACTIVITY as a fun way to wrap up the week.

TOWERS OF LIGHT

LIGHT OF MINE

WEEK ONE
SHINING LIGHT

Memory Verse:
"Let your light so shine before men, that they may see your good works, and glorify your Father which is in heaven."
—Matthew 5:16

LIGHT
OF
MINE

VOCABULARY

WORD LIST

As part of your daily work this week, you'll need to use a dictionary and a thesaurus to look up definitions, synonyms, and antonyms for the words below.

CADRE

CONTEMPLATE

MERCENARY

CERAMIC

LOFT

MUTE

SECRET MESSAGE

This week's vocabulary words have been used to form the message below, but it's been encrypted to keep it a secret. Determine which letter in the alphabet corresponds to each number to decode the message.

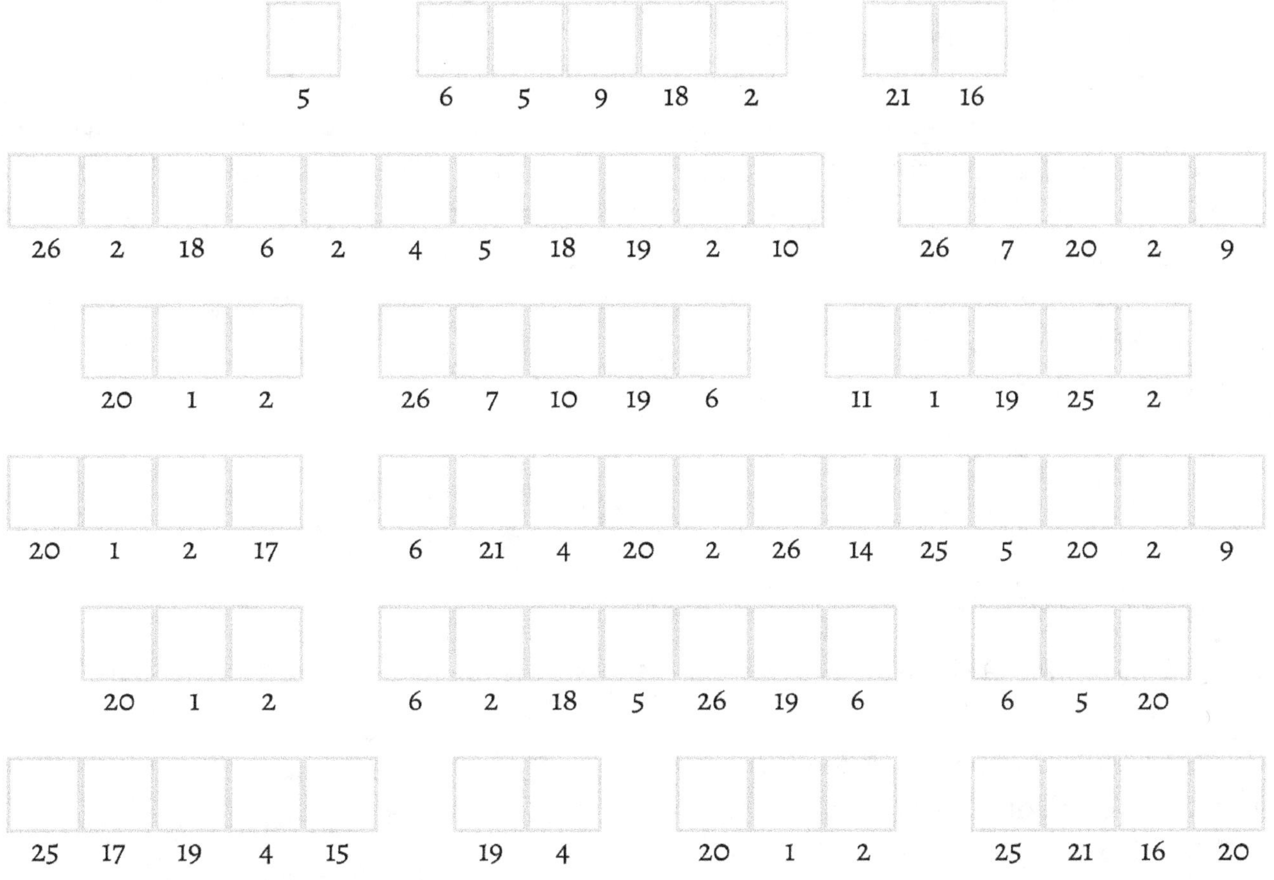

DAY ONE

MEMORY VERSE & VOCABULARY

In your reading journal, copy this week's memory verse and vocabulary definitions.

STORY PASSAGE

After a delicious meal of Mother's fried chicken, mashed potatoes, green beans, and biscuits, the Parson wiped his mouth and said, "Children, your father tells me you are more diligent than the ants of the field. You have built a solid tower in record time."

"Thank you, Sir!" exclaimed the children.

The Parson rose from the table. "There is just one thing missing."

"What?" asked Ethan, echoing what Lauren was thinking. Father's plans were so detailed. She couldn't imagine what they'd missed.

The Parson bent over and picked up his sack, then he removed a metal lantern and set it on the table. "The Light, of course."

The lantern was a dull bronze color that reminded Lauren of the brass knockers on the church door. It looked about five hands high and one hand wide. The glass faces had a golden stained-glass cross in the center of each face. She really loved that because it reminded her of the stained-glass window in her grandma's great room. The lantern held no candle, but a small spike protruded from its center.

Aiden set his elbows on the table and leaned closer. "Mama, will you get a candle, so we can light it?"

The Parson patted Aiden on the head. "Son, not for this lantern."

WHERE DO YOU THINK THE LANTERN'S LIGHT COMES FROM?

CHAPTER READING QUESTIONS

Read chapter one and then answer the following questions in your reading journal.

1. Why does Father build the tower?
2. What special animals visit the farm?
3. What does Father do for work?
4. Are the Mighty Mercenaries trustworthy? Why or why not?
5. Where does the light for the tower come from?

Joke of the Day

Why did the scarecrow win an award
He was out-STANDING in his field!

DAY TWO

MEMORY VERSE & VOCABULARY

In your reading journal, copy this week's memory verse and list three synonyms for each vocabulary word.

STORY PASSAGE

"Aiden thinks it was the Dark One. 'Cause he says Daddy put the lightning rods up, and the lightning hit where it wasn't supposed to." Ethan's chin lifted as he showed pride in his brother. Ethan fisted his right hand and shook it toward the window. "I'm gonna conk the Dark One on his wonkus for making us carry all that water and for taking my Daddy away."

Lauren's lips tightened. "Ethan, I don't think you'll be going after the Dark One anytime soon."

"In the Good Book, a little boy, who had God on his side, beat a giant that scared a whole army." Ethan declared. "If God wants us to go save Daddy, we will."

"Young Ethan, you are exactly right. The Good Book is full of examples where the Spirit of the Lord helps an unlikely person defeat evil." The Parson pointed toward the great room, where Father's copy of the Good Book was visible. "If you read carefully, you will discover more miracles like this in its pages. You will see them in your own life only if the Lord calls you to them." He clasped his hands together. "So, young Ethan, I hope you ask God to go with you before you go conking any wonkuses. OK?"

"Yes sir," Ethan said as he looked down at his plate with a pout on his lips.

WHAT BIBLE STORY IS ETHAN REFERRING TO?

CHAPTER READING QUESTIONS

1. Read chapter two and then answer the following questions in your reading journal.

1. What does Mother do during the storm?
2. What does Aiden think hit the windmill? Why?
3. Why did Aiden think the Dark One was responsible for the broken windmill?
4. What may have led to Father's disapperance?
5. Who does Mother say will help the children?

Joke of the Day

Why can't a giant sloth drive a car?
Because they're extinct.

DAY THREE

MEMORY VERSE & VOCABULARY

In your reading journal, copy this week's memory verse and list three antonyms for each vocabulary word.

STORY PASSAGE

Lauren came inside and said excitedly, "I found the last bit of ham!"

This distracted Aiden. As he pushed the pot further into the fireplace, a foot spike caught on a gap in the bricks, and it tipped toward the fire; water cascaded out. Before Aiden could correct his movement, the spider pot tipped further, and the lid slid off, crashing into the flames and scattering the wood inside the fireplace.

The fire hissed and snapped as liquid engulfed it. Before Aiden's eyes, the water extinguished his beautiful fire.

Lauren rushed up to try to help Aiden, ham in hand. Then the whole thing backwashed ashy water and partially burnt sticks out of the fireplace and all down Aiden's shirt.

The floor was already wet from Ethan's spill, and the ashy sludge added to the slippery mess. Lauren's leather-bottomed shoes slid, and she prevented herself from falling by dropping the slab of meat and catching the side of the oven. The ham landed with a plop in the middle of the ashy slime.

At the same time, more smoke and steam than could be handled by the flue billowed out of the oven, cloaking the kitchen into momentary darkness as it obscured the light from the window.

WHAT CHOICES AFFECT THE LIGHT WITHIN US LIKE THE FIRE'S FLAME?

CHAPTER READING QUESTIONS

Read chapter three and then answer the following questions in your reading journal.

1. What did Lauren use to organize the work?
2. Who is Ethan's special friend?
3. What little accomplishment made Ethan very proud?
4. How did Lauren react to the fire begin put out?

Joke of the Day

Who's the king of the woodshop?

The ruler!

DAY FOUR

MEMORY VERSE & VOCABULARY

In your reading journal, copy this week's memory verse and draw a picture definition for each vocabulary word.

STORY PASSAGE

Finally, Lauren said, "Let me try." She reached for the rod, and as her fingers wrapped around it, she felt a sensation like warm water running over her arms. The weapon handle reduced in width to more comfortably fit her hand. Then one end formed a spear tip made of an aquamarine glow around the metal tip. Indeed, the whole spear glowed with a light that flowed like water. As Lauren gripped the weapon with both hands, the radiance ran over her fingers, as did the watery aura.

"Whoa!" Aiden took a step back from Lauren. "That's amazing."

"Aiden, I'll bet that's for you." Lauren set the base of the spear on the floor and pointed to the sword with her other hand. "I never touched that, and it didn't move when E tripped over it. I'll bet it's yours."

Aiden reached for the sword hilt. The instant he touched it, he said, "I feel a fire in my chest." The sword shrank from a two-handed longsword for a grown up to the size of a short sword that Aiden could wield in a two-handed grip.

A blue-white flame burst out along the sword handle, startling Aiden, who dropped it. The Fire disappeared, and the sword returned to its full size as it clattered to the floor.

"Oops," he said, red-faced. Then he picked it up more carefully, and the fire returned.

WHAT POWERS THE CHILDREN'S WEAPONS?

CHAPTER READING QUESTIONS

Read chapter four and then answer the following questions in your reading journal.

1. Who is Aiden's special friend?
2. Who comes to visit the children?
3. Who was supposed to visit the children?
4. What tool does Aiden use to fix the windmill?
5. What is the theme of the stories Lauren reads in the Good Book?

Joke of the Day

Did you hear the rumor about butter? Nevermind, I shouldn't spread it.

DAY FIVE

READING & MEMORY VERSE

Read chapter five in the book. Then, recite this week's memory verse aloud and complete the activity below. Include the coloring page and vocabulary puzzle with today's activities.

ACTIVITY: LANTERN

MATERIALS

- An empty cereal box (or similiar box)
- Wax paper & plastic wrap
- Construction paper
- Scissors
- Tape
- Markers

INSTRUCTIONS

Carefully open the flaps on both ends of the ceral box and cut along the edge of one corner to open the box fully. (The box will be refolded and taped back together with the inside facing out.) Cut openings in the front and back panels of the ceral box.

Next, cut sheets of wax paper and plastic wrap to be a little larger than the openings cut into the front and back of the cereal box. (These will be the "glass panes" of the lantern.) Use construction paper to cut out two identical candles and flames (one for each opening). Tape one flame to the top of each candle and draw a black line from the flame to the candle for the wick.

Then, flip the box over so the printed side is up and the cardboard side is down. Tape a sheet of plastic wrap over each opening. Then, tape a candle on top of the plastic in each opening (make sure the candle can be seen from the other side of the box). Tape the wax paper on top of the candle and the plastic wrap so that it can be seen behind the candle from the cardboard side of the box.

Last, flip the box over to write this week's memory verse on the cardboard side and decorate the box. Tape the box back together with the cardboard side facing out.

WEEK TWO
FACING TRIALS

Memory Verse:
"But when they deliver you up, take no thought how or what ye shall speak: for it shall be given you in that same hour what ye shall speak. For it is not ye that speak, but the Spirit of your Father which speaketh in you."
—Matthew 10:19-20

LAUREN

VOCABULARY

WORD LIST

As part of your daily work this week, you'll need to use a dictionary and a thesaurus to look up definitions, synonyms, and antonyms for the words below.

CONGREGANT   REGAL   SACRAMENT
HERETIC   RITUAL   SANCTUARY

WORD SCRAMBLE

Rearrange each group of letters below to unscramble the words.

AREONTGGNC

__ __ __ __ __ __ __ __ __ __

ACRASYNUT

__ __ __ __ __ __ __ __ __

CREHTIE

__ __ __ __ __ __ __

CNATRSEMA

__ __ __ __ __ __ __ __ __

LERGA

__ __ __ __ __

AIUTLR

__ __ __ __ __ __

DAY ONE

MEMORY VERSE

In your reading journal, copy this week's memory verse and vocabulary definitions.

STORY PASSAGE

"Heretic! This message you spew, 'tolerate others' beliefs, no matter how they behave or what they do,' is not the message of the Good Book!"

Lauren's limbs stiffened. What on earth had just happened? Never in the middle of a sermon had someone stood to disagree about what was or was not in the Good Book. Who was telling the truth, this finely dressed bishop or this raggedy old man, seemingly a knight protector?

The old man stepped toward the front of the church and turned to look at the congregation. "Have you been to Loggerton?" He punctuated each word with a pound of his staff against the floor. The thud, thud, echoed in Lauren's ears, making her wince. "Have you seen how the Darkness has gripped that community?"

Silence reigned in the chapel. Lauren could not take her eyes off the old man. Something deep inside her confirmed his words, his tone, his anger. Plus, he wore the colors of Father's cadre. Her throat tightened. If only Father were here to confirm who spoke the truth.

The battered knight protector threw his arms in the air and raised his face, as if toward the heavens. "The Good Book's message is to love God with all your heart and then love others! You cannot love God and tolerate evil!"

WHAT DOES LOVING OTHERS WITHOUT TOLERATING EVIL LOOK LIKE?

CHAPTER READING QUESTIONS

Read chapter six and then answer the following questions in your reading journal.

1. Why are the kids excited to see the Parson?
2. What stands out about the countryside on the way to the church?
3. Why was Ethan acting strange when he returned to the church service?
4. Who storms out of the church service? Why?

Joke of the Day

Why don't oysters share their pearls?
Because they're shellfish.

DAY TWO

MEMORY VERSE

In your reading journal, copy this week's memory verse and list three synonyms for each vocabulary word.

STORY PASSAGE

"Silence, child!" the Bishop barked. As he turned back to Lauren and Aiden, his fearsome expression melted into calm, as if the incident with Ethan had not occurred. "Despite their best efforts to keep your mother from running headlong into danger, the Mighty Mercenaries have lost contact with her. The Bishop stood up and motioned out the window as if pointing toward the tower. "With both parents missing, there is a great concern for the Tower of Light." While its power naturally keeps the Darkness at bay, it's vulnerable to vandalism without someone to guard and protect it."

Aiden perked up. "We can guard it! We have magic weapons. Mine is a fiery sword."

"I'm sure you have all kinds of magic," the Bishop assured in a patronizing tone. "What is needed now is more than good intentions and your active imagination. Did I not already have to reprimand your brother about asking permission properly before speaking?" The Bishop stood and pointed to another corner in the room. "In fact, you go there now, and contemplate the ways to show proper respect for your elders."

Lauren could no longer sit still and watch her brothers being punished for speaking truth. She again clasped her hands and faced the Bishop. "Good Bishop, may I speak, Your Holiness, sir?"

WHY DO YOU THINK LAUREN REACTED THE WAY SHE DID?

CHAPTER READING QUESTIONS

Read chapter seven and then answer the following questions in your reading journal.

1. What does Sparkle Frog do that's so amazing?
2. How are the children treated after church?
3. What item is sent with the children?
4. What document is shown to the children?
5. Who returns home with the children?

Joke of the Day

The invisible man turned down a job.
He couldn't see himself doing it.

DAY THREE

MEMORY VERSE

In your reading journal, copy this week's memory verse and list three antonyms for each vocabulary word.

STORY PASSAGE

As the children walked home, Aiden was really confused about what had just transpired. He got that Lauren was just trying to get them out of a sticky situation, but this didn't feel right to him. He turned back toward the church. "Sissy, look behind us! The sky still isn't right. Why hasn't it lit up?"

The Violet Acolyte swelled with pride. "The Bishop says the Darkness is spreading. Soon, the twilight will bathe all of Zoura. That's why the Bishop's here. If you notice, the haze fades just outside the church. This concerns the Bishop greatly."

"Let me see if I understand." Aiden took the lead as the acolyte didn't know where to turn toward their home. "The Bishop thinks the Darkness has spread to the church and he's trying to figure out how that could have happened?"

Aiden began walking backward to continue the conversation. He knew this road like the back of his hand, and there was something shifty about this guy. He wanted to get the whole story.

The acolyte nodded at Aiden's assertion, his expression earnest. "Something like that."

DO YOU THINK THE ACOLYTE IS BEING TRUTHFUL OR DECEPTIVE?

CHAPTER READING QUESTIONS

Read chapter eight and then answer the following questions in your reading journal.

1. What does the sky look like on the way home? What does it mean?
2. What does the acolyte think of the Parson?
3. How does the acolyte react to meeting Daddy Duck?
4. What happened to the tower while the children were gone?

Joke of the Day

What did the boyscout say when he got back from his trip to the general store?

Supplies!

DAY FOUR

MEMORY VERSE

In your reading journal, copy this week's memory verse and draw a picture definition for each vocabulary word.

STORY PASSAGE

Lauren stepped forward. "Since you're not from here, I can understand you not knowing our song, but how can you not know about keeping the Sabbath?"

"Oh, that." The acolyte shook his head dismissively. "Child, when you have studied the Good Book as I have, under the tutelage of the best scholars, you begin to understand what it really means." He put his hand to his chest and sighed. "The strict rules of the Old Book do not apply to us believers of the New Book We are unbound from the rules of the first followers of God." The acolyte pointed to the Good Book next to Father's chair in the great room. "If you knew your Good Book well, you'd know that even the Savior 'worked' on the Sabbath by healing a man." He made a showing motion with his hands. "Go! Do what I asked so we can have a proper meal."

"Daddy wouldn't like this." Ethan squared his shoulders and made fists. "I don't know about all the things you're talking about, but I'm not going to do something Daddy wouldn't like."

"Me, neither," Aiden declared, stepping between Ethan and the acolyte. Ethan was proud of his big brother stepping up to defend him.

"I'm with my brothers," Lauren said as she stepped next to Aiden.

WHAT DOES "KEEPING THE SABBATH" MEAN?

CHAPTER READING QUESTIONS

Read chapter nine and then answer the following questions in your reading journal.

1. What did the acolyte not know about the Light?
2. What did the acolyte eat for lunch and why did it surprise the children?
3. What does Meow Meow decide to play with?
4. Why did the acolyte apologize?

Joke of the Day

My uncle's dogs are Timex and Rolex. They are his WATCH dogs!

DAY FIVE

READING & MEMORY VERSE

Read chapter ten in the book. Then, recite this week's memory verse aloud and complete the activity below. Include the coloring page and vocabulary puzzle with today's activities.

ACTIVITY: KALEIDOSCOPE

MATERIALS

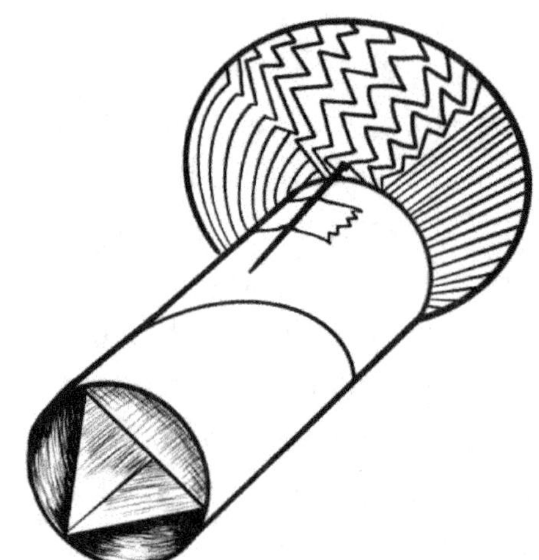

- An empty toilet paper tube
- A 3x5 index card
- Aluminum foil
- 4 inch white paper circle
- Markers
- Toothpick
- Tape

INSTRUCTIONS

Fold the index card into a three-sided triangle that fits snuggly into the toilet paper tube (adjust as needed). Then, unfold the index card and wrap it in aluminum foil. Make sure the smooth, shiny side is on the inside of the triangle. Refold, securing the aluminum foil and triangle with tape. Insert the triangle into the toilet paper tube.

Using markers, decorate the outside of the tube and color 3-4 patterns on the white paper circle. Next, place a small piece of tape in the middle on the backside of the white paper circle. Then, poke the toothpick through the center of the white paper circle—going through the tape on the backside. (The paper circle should rotate freely around the toothpick.) Tape the other end of the toothpick to one end of the toilet paper tube.

Holding the kaleidoscope up to the light, look through the open end of the toilet paper tube while turning the white paper circle on the opposite end.

WHAT HAPPENS TO THE VIEW WHEN YOU TURN THE KALEIDOSCOPE?
HOW CAN WE CHANGE OUR VIEW WHEN FACING TRAILS?

WEEK THREE
ARMOR OF GOD

Memory Verse:
"Above all, taking the shield of faith, wherewith ye shall be able to quench all the fiery darts of the wicked. And take the helmet of salvation, and the sword of the Spirit, which is the word of God:"
—Ephesians 6:16-17 KJV

AIDEN

VOCABULARY

WORD LIST

As part of your daily work this week, you'll need to use a dictionary and a thesaurus to look up definitions, synonyms, and antonyms for the words below.

ACOLYTE   FIDDLE   PROTECTOR
ETCH   ILLUMINATE

MAZE

Help the kids escape! Trace a path from the center of the maze to the outside.

DAY ONE

MEMORY VERSE

In your reading journal, copy this week's memory verse and vocabulary definitions.

STORY PASSAGE

In the kitchen, Aiden started a fire, and Ethan got the slate and some chalk so Lauren could write a note:

THANK YOU FOR HELPING US.
WE WENT TO PICK BERRIES AS A SPECIAL TREAT FOR YOU. PLEASE WATER AND
FEED THE ANIMALS WHILE WE ARE GONE. WE WILL BE BACK SOON.

As she dotted the period, she could sense the light from the tower dimming. They "were" going to get berries, so it wasn't a lie, was it? Should they really be doing this?

"C'mon, Sissy, we need to make sure Sparkle Frog can't be hurt by the dark water." Ethan said as he tugged on her dress.

Lauren looked down on her brother. His earnest look convinced her to stay the course. But would God really help them when they needed it if they were lying?

Lauren wiped the slate clean and the light grew slightly brighter.

"Sissy? Why did you do that?" Aiden asked.

Lauren took a deep breath and slowly let it out. "We can't start a mission for the Light under the cloud of a lie."

WHY DOES THE LIGHT DIM WHEN LAUREN WRITES THE NOTE?

CHAPTER READING QUESTIONS

Read chapter eleven and then answer the following questions in your reading journal.

1. What wakes the children up?
2. Where does the quest for the source of the dark water take the children?
3. What do the children find there?
4. What amazing things destroy the darkness?
5. Who do the children see as they flee?

Joke of the Day

Have you ever eaten zucchini noodles?
Me either. I don't like impastas.

DAY TWO

MEMORY VERSE

In your reading journal, copy this week's memory verse and list three synonyms for each vocabulary word.

STORY PASSAGE

Lauren turned to Ethan, "Whatever it is, it can wait until later. We have chores to do." Ethan was very frustrated by this. *We need to tell to make the Light bright.*

"But Sissy!" Ethan demanded

"We'll finish the chores!" Lauren commanded sternly. She picked up the silver bowl in her right hand while she held the broom in her left. "Aiden, now that we are home, you should put the knife Father gave you away with the other special things like this silver bowl."

"Put my knife away?" Aiden asked with a raised eyebrow.

"Yes, in the trunk, upstairs." Lauren waved the bowl in Aiden's direction, so a reflection showed a light spot on his face. "We shouldn't leave this out."

"Oh yeah, the trunk," Aiden said as he hustled to follow Lauren into the great room. "E, can you help Brother Flower with the eggs?"

Ethan was very concerned about them not being fully honest with Brother Flower, but he could tell by the way his siblings were emphasizing certain words that they must be trying to talk in code. They did that sometimes, and he could never really follow them.

WHAT ARE SOME WAYS TO AVOID REVEALING SOMETHING THAT SHOULDN'T BE REVEALED WITHOUT LYING?

CHAPTER READING QUESTIONS

Read chapter twelve and then answer the following questions in your reading journal.

1. What do the children bring to the acolyte?
2. Who visited the house and why?
3. What was added to the tower?

Joke of the Day

Why did the cat go to the hospital?
To get a CAT-scan.

DAY THREE

MEMORY VERSE

In your reading journal, copy this week's memory verse and list three antonyms for each vocabulary word.

STORY PASSAGE

She stood at the window, begging God to give her wisdom. Then she felt drawn to pick up the broom that had been her spear. As her hand wrapped around the middle of its shaft, an aqua-colored light flowed over her hand and up and down the shaft—as it had done when she'd picked up the spear for the first time. The radiance reached the top of the shaft, extended almost a forearm's length beyond the end of the it, and culminated in a sharp spear point. Simultaneously, the straw making it a broom disappeared. Spear in hand, she glanced out the window once again.

The Knight Protector had gained an advantage on the Violet Acolyte and backed him into a corner. As Lauren watched in horror, he knocked the hammer from the acolyte's hand. The acolyte cried out, then reached for his horn.

Lauren's lips tightened. She prayed, pulled back her arm, and froze. Could she really throw the spear hard enough to hurt a man wearing armor? Then she remembered Aiden's sword. If it could cut through hinges and locks, her spear should be able to stop the him.

She hurled the spear with all her might and watched it fly through the air. Just as it reached the window of the tower, the Knight Protector stepped aside, which put the acolyte's head in the direct path of the spear.

HOW WILL BEING STRUCK BY THE SPEAR AFFECT THE ACOLYTE?

CHAPTER READING QUESTIONS

Read chapter thirteen and then answer the following questions in your reading journal.

1. What happens when Lauren uses her spear?
2. What happens to the Knight Protector?
3. Who do the kids find in the tower?
4. What does Ethan find along the way?

Joke of the Day

A skunk fell in my swimming pool?
Yep, he stank right to the bottom.

DAY FOUR

MEMORY VERSE

In your reading journal, copy this week's memory verse and draw a picture definition for each vocabulary word.

STORY PASSAGE

Aiden unwound the loop of rope, while Ethan went back to the barn. *I sure hope he'll actually get the sacks of grain and not just fool around in the mud. There's no telling when the storm will break, and I wouldn't want the Knight Protector to catch us while we're doing this.*

The top of the Tower of Light had a square-shaped hole about the width of two grain sacks that allowed light to pass all the way down to the floor. A wooden railing that came to Aiden's waist surrounded the hole, with a pole at each corner and another pole halfway in between. From the top, it was a straight shot to ground level. The light illuminated everything inside, including the stairs, so there was no need for torches.

Aiden took the rope off his shoulder and tied one end to the railing at the top of the tower. Then he dropped the rest of the coil of rope down the hole. As he walked down the stairs, he saw the old torches on either side of the door. They had used them when building the tower. Since they never used them anymore, the torches were covered with dust and cobwebs.

Ethan returned to the tower as Aiden took a torch from the wall. Aiden hated the way the cobwebs felt when they stuck to his hand. He swapped hands and wiped the dirty one on his wet pants. Then Aiden patted Ethan on the head as he passed, saying, "Good job."

HOW DO YOU KNOW WHEN NOT TO SAY SOMETHING ALOUD?

CHAPTER READING QUESTIONS

Read chapter fourteen and then answer the following questions in your reading journal.

1. What do the children decide to do about the Knight Protector?
2. Describe the trap the children set up.

Joke of the Day

How do you fix a flat pumpkin?
With a pumpkin patch.

DAY FIVE

READING & MEMORY VERSE

Read chapter fifteen in the book. Then, recite this week's memory verse aloud and complete the activity below. Include the coloring page and vocabulary puzzle with today's activities.

ACTIVITY: EGGS-PERIMENT

MATERIALS

- An egg
- Vinegar
- A jar or container large enough to place the egg inside

INSTRUCTIONS

Place the egg inside the container. Fill the container with enough vinegar to cover the egg. Let it sit overnight.

The next day, you will notice the egg's hard outer shell is gone. Only the thin inner membrane is keeping the egg intact. This change is known as a chemical change. The acetic acid in the vinegar interacted with the calcium carbonate in the egg's shell to create a carbonic acid and calcium acetate. Then, the carbonic acid broke down to become carbon dioxide and water.

HOW IS SIN IN OUR LIVES LIKE WHAT HAPPENED TO THE EGG?

WEEK FOUR
HOLY SPIRIT

Memory Verse:

"Then Samuel took the horn of oil, and anointed him in the midst of his brethren: and the Spirit of the Lord came upon David from that day forward. So Samuel rose up, and went to Ramah."

1 Samuel 16:13 KJV

ETHAN

VOCABULARY

WORD LIST

As part of your daily work this week, you'll need to use a dictionary and a thesaurus to look up definitions, synonyms, and antonyms for the words below.

DISARM   MESMERIZE   TASSEL
INTRUDER   SORCERY

WORD SEARCH

Find and circle the hidden vocabulary words in the puzzle below. Words may appear up, down, forwards, backwards, or diagonally.

ACOLYTE   ETCH   MERCENARY   SACRAMENT
CADRE   FIDDLE   MESMERIZE   SANCTUARY
CERAMIC   HERETIC   MUTED   SORCERY
CONGREGANT   ILLUMINATE   PROTECTOR   TASSEL
CONTEMPLATE   INTRUDER   REGAL
DISARM   LOFT   RITUAL

```
C S A C R A M E N T H P F L M P H F B K G C W C L
I P Z C S S P R B K R M J A I E R E L E O W L O O
M A A O Y K O O A O L M Z G K U R E S N F A W N C
A G D V E F P R T C Y M I E A R S C G M U S I T S
R D I S A R M E C V O H N R L S O R E T A M F E E
E M T R R V C W Y E P L B Q A D E S I N B T I M Z
C Y R A U T C N A S R D Y T H G D R R L A F G P I
W I H D O Q C F T W E Y A T A O I I P Q W R G L R
U F T R H A T F B S V K L N E N N U F G Q B Y A E
G A A E I T O E Z F T Y T M A Y T F A X V P L T M
T U B O R L J X R Q P V X U Q G R E M U T E D E S
R B I X R E T A N I M U L L I F U W R D V T C Y E
X Y U A B B H X K K R Z M Q X O D V X D C C E U M
X Y B A R Z Y S G N C Z R X J P E I I I A H D Q A
U G F N R S S G D X F B G D O V R T J K I C O X W
```

DAY ONE

MEMORY VERSE

In your reading journal, copy this week's memory verse and vocabulary definitions.

STORY PASSAGE

"No!" Aiden cried as the deadly blade came down. From the corner of his eye, he saw Ethan curl up in a ball under his shield as Lauren reached to pick up her spear from where she'd set it against the wall.

Time seemed to slow as Aiden gripped his sword and the fire welled up in his chest and down his arm. He finished his draw, and the blue-white flames engulfed the blade as the acolyte's sword descended point first toward the knight's chest.

Aiden hit the flat of the acolyte's blade with the flat of his own and swept up and to the left. Aiden's blade slid up the side of the acolyte's weapon until the flames on Aiden's sword began to burn the acolyte, and he dropped the sword.

"What sorcery is this?" the acolyte yelled as he blew on his burnt fingers.
Blue-green liquid energy surrounded Lauren's staff, which she used to sweep the acolyte's legs out from under him.

He fell to his knees. "Why would you prevent me from destroying a minion of darkness. . . unless you are the Darkness yourselves?" the acolyte spat.

Ethan popped his head out from beneath his shield. "Killing is a trait of the Darkness. The Good Book says, 'Thou shalt not kill.'" The little boy got up and dusted himself off and stood with his hands balled in fists on his hips.

WHAT ARE THE OTHER TRAITS OF DARKNESS (OR THE FLESH)?

CHAPTER READING QUESTIONS

Read chapter sixteen and then answer the following questions in your reading journal.

1. Did the children's trap work? Who got caught?
2. What does the acolyte want to do to the knight?
3. What heroic act does Ethan do?
4. How does the knight explain his behavior?
5. What happens when the acolyte blows his horn?

Joke of the Day

What do you call a sword made of ice?
Excali-burrrrrr.

DAY TWO

MEMORY VERSE

In your reading journal, copy this week's memory verse and list three synonyms for each vocabulary word.

STORY PASSAGE

The narrow beam of light coming from the house allowed him to notice the engraving of the Lantern of Light on his shield. It began to glow ever so softly. A memory of Father rose from the present chaos. . .

They'd gathered around the kitchen table, on which had been set the lantern from the Tower of Light.

Father pointed at Ethan's chest. "The light for this lantern is inside of each of us."

Ethan looked down at his chest, then threw his hands in the air. "I don't see the light, Daddy."

"When you love the Lord with all your heart, mind, and soul, the Good Book says you reflect the Savior's Light on the world." Father patted Ethan's head. "Would you like to learn a song about how we can shine that light?"

Ethan stood up and stepped forward, away from the kitchen door. His memory echoed the same words the old Knight Protector had just yelled. With the Light, he could stand on his own. He could fight the Darkness. He had the Light. Of course! He'd had it all the time! The hounds crept closer, closer. "This little light of mine, I'm gonna let it shine."

WHAT IS THE LIGHT ETHAN HAS AND WHERE DOES IT COME FROM?

CHAPTER READING QUESTIONS

Read chapter seventeen and then answer the following questions in your reading journal.

1. What advice does the knight give Ethan?
2. What happens when the acolyte tries to help?
3. What does the Holy Spirit's power allow their weapons to do?
4. Is the censer more powerful than the lantern?
5. What happens to the Bishop?

Joke of the Day

Which vegetable is the most loving?
An artichoke. It has a heart.

DAY THREE

MEMORY VERSE

In your reading journal, copy this week's memory verse and list three antonyms for each vocabulary word.

STORY PASSAGE

"I feel such pain." A cough tore through a faint whisper, making him hard to understand. "Call. . . call me Nicholas. That's my given name. I. . . I no longer serve what I now know was the Darkness."

The Knight Protector, still supported by Aiden, came near and visibly winced at the scene as he managed to kneel on one knee and put his arm around Ethan, whose sobs had not diminished. "Son, the acolyte is not long for this world."

"His name is Nicholas," Lauren said solemnly.

"The only hope for Nicholas now is God's mercy," said the Knight Protector.

"OK." Ethan wiped away tears and sat straighter. "Let's pray." He bowed his head; the others did the same. "Dear God, please help Nicholas." As he prayed, sniffles punctuated his words. "Please, please fix him, God. He is a good friend, and he saved Sissy and Aiden. He saved Sparkle Frog. He saved me, too." Please, God!" Ethan's voice rang out with the depth and confidence of the young child of faith that he was. "Please save Nicholas."

The Lantern of Light grew brighter, and a light haloed Nicholas's head.

"I have been saved. . . from the Darkness. You children have shown me the Light."

WHAT DOES NICOLAS MEAN WHEN HE SAYS, "I HAVE BEEN SAVED"?
WHAT DOES SALVATION MEAN TO YOU?

CHAPTER READING QUESTIONS

Read chapter eighteen and then answer the following questions in your reading journal.

1. What did the children do to help the acolyte?
   Did it work, why or why not?

DAY FOUR

MEMORY VERSE

In your reading journal, copy this week's memory verse and draw a picture definition for each vocabulary word.

STORY PASSAGE

"Ethan, your light is so very bright." Tears rolled down her lovely face, and she began to cry. "I saw it last night! It was so glorious, and undoubtedly cause for celebration, but you must not tarry at home. You must take your light to the far corners of the land and light the other towers.

"The forces of Darkness are after you!" Mother continued. "Their lord, the Dark One, comes again for you. Seek help from the Knight Protector. Father shared his plans to shine the Light from Blooming Glen with him." Her eyes glistened like they held diamonds, so brilliant were her tears. "You must shine your light over the whole wide world! Let it shine."

A shadow passed over the beam of light: Mother was gone. Ethan now saw an image of a man in a cage wearing an iron mask. He was bound to the bars with iron restraints. Ethan began to shake. Despite the cover, Ethan knew precisely who he was: their father.

"Daddy! I'll shine my light and save you!" Ethan pleaded with the darkness, "Sissy, Aiden and me will shine our light over the whole, wide world."

HOW CAN YOU SHINE YOUR LIGHT BEFORE OTHERS?

CHAPTER READING QUESTIONS

Read chapter nineteen and then answer the following questions in your reading journal.

1. Where was Mother?

Joke of the Day

Do you know why marsupials aren't allowed to have a drivers license? They don't have the KOALA-fications

DAY FIVE

READING & MEMORY VERSE

Read chapter twenty in the book. Then, recite this week's memory verse aloud and complete the activity below. Include the coloring page and vocabulary puzzle with today's activities.

ACTIVITY: PLANTING

MATERIALS

- An empty plastic water bottle with cap
- 4 inches of yarn
- One cup of potting soil
- Seeds (Tip: beans, peas, or sunflowers work best)
- Scissors

INSTRUCTIONS

Cut the plastic bottle in half. Make sure there is about an inch of space between the cap and the bottom of the bottle when the top half of the bottle is inserted upside down into the bottom half.

Next, remove the cap and poke a hole in the center of it. Tie a knot in one end of the yarn and thread it through the hole in the cap (with the knot on the inside). Screw the cap on.

Then, pour water into the bottom half of the bottle (at least an inch or so deep). Place the top half of the bottle upside down into the bottom half. (The string should be touching the bottom of the bottle and the bottle cap should be submerged.) Fill the top half of the bottle with soil, leaving at least an inch of space between the soil and the rim of the bottle.

Last, gently plant the seed into the soil and place it where the plant will get plently of sunlight. Be sure to refill the water in the bottom of the bottle as necessary.

HOW IS THE PLANT LIKE OUR FAITH?

STILL SMALL VOICE

WEEK ONE
A SMALL VOICE

Memory Verse:
"And after the earthquake a fire; but the LORD was not in the fire: and after the fire a still small voice."
—1 Kings 19:12 KJV

AIDEN

VOCABULARY

WORD LIST

As part of your daily work this week, you'll need to use a dictionary and a thesaurus to look up definitions, synonyms, and antonyms for the words below.

CRESCENDO   METAPHOR   PROLOGUE
LACQUER   PANTOMIME   SILHOUETTE

SECRET MESSAGE

This week's vocabulary words have been used to form the message below, but it's been encrypted to keep it a secret. Determine which letter in the alphabet corresponds to each number to decode the message.

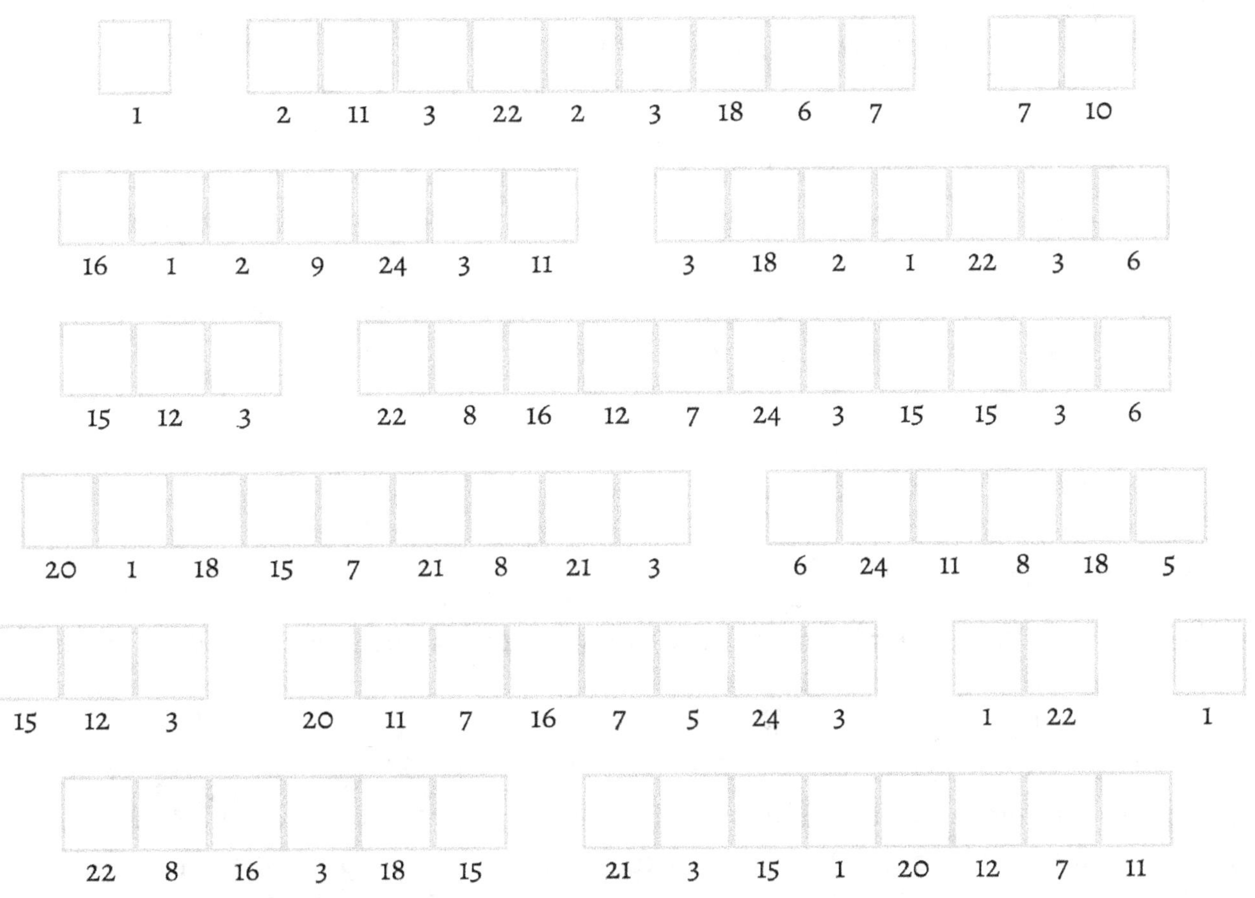

DAY ONE

MEMORY VERSE, VOCABULARY & READING

In your reading journal, copy this week's memory verse and vocabulary definitions. Then, read chapters one and two in the book.

STORY PASSAGE

Knight Protector continued, "This is all so very complicated. But it is clear you are all clever and keep your own counsel on what is best." The warrior rubbed the top of his head.

Ethan winced. *We really conked him in his wonkus last night.*

"You will not just obey me because I am your elder." The old knight looked to each of the children staring into their eyes. "With the deception of the bishop and even my own behavior, it has to be difficult for you to trust anyone. Oh… where to begin." Knight Protector sighed.

"Pray!" Ethan blurted out. He had a plate of bacon and flapjacks in front of him, and his stomach was aching.

"What?" Knight Protector sat back in his chair, wide-eyed at this.

"You said you didn't know where to begin. Daddy always says when you don't know what to do, pray." Ethan folded his hands together. "Plus, we can't eat if we don't pray, and I'm starving."

"You are right, of course. This is your home and your table. Would you want to ask for the Lord's blessing for us?" Knight Protector asked.

HAVE YOU EVER PRAYED FOR GUIDENCE?

PASSAGE QUESTIONS

Read the STORY PASSAGE and answer the following questions in your reading journal.

1. What does the Knight Protector mean when he says "keep your own counsel"?
2. Which sentence supports the previous answer?
3. When Ethan tells the Knight Protector to pray, what do you think he is most concerned about?
4. Which sentence supports the previous answer?

Joke of the Day

Have you heard Optimus Prime is writing a book?
It's an AUTOBOT-ography.

DAY TWO

MEMORY VERSE, VOCABULARY & READING

In your reading journal, copy this week's memory verse and list three synonyms for each vocabulary word. Then, read chapters three and four in the book.

STORY PASSAGE

Aiden wasn't buying it. *I don't think the Lord would let bad stuff go on if a warrior like the Knight Protector could do something about it.* Aiden balled his fists and put them on his hips. "But, if the small voice told you to find the Darkness machine, why didn't you knock it down before we got there?"

Knight Protector leaned forward in his chair with his hands on the arms and looked straight at Aiden. "It was the Spirit's promptings that helped me to find the Darkness generator. Then, the still small voice told me to wait and see. And low and behold, I saw a young boy wield the sword of Gabriel and smite the Darkness. That was a most glorious sight indeed."

"The sword of Gabriel? You mean the archangel Gabriel from the good book?" Lauren blurted out unexpectedly. This caused Aiden to take a step back.

"Well, maybe not 'the' sword of Gabriel. It stands watch over the garden. But a fiery sword of the type only wielded by the angels." Knight Protector patted the Good Book to emphasize his point.

Aiden's mind swirled at the thought that his sword may have been wielded by angels.

HOW DO YOU KNOW WHEN THE HOLY SPIRIT IS GUIDING YOU?

PASSAGE QUESTIONS

Read the STORY PASSAGE and answer the following questions in your reading journal.

1. What did the Knight Protector discover?
2. How did Aiden feel about the Knight Protector's choice of action regarding the discovery?
3. Which sentence supports the previous answer?
4. Why did the Knight Protector choose the action he took?

> **Joke of the Day**
>
> Want to hear a joke about a piece of paper?
>
> Nevermind. It's tear-able.

DAY THREE

MEMORY VERSE, VOCABULARY & READING

In your reading journal, copy this week's memory verse and list three antonyms for each vocabulary word. Then, read chapters five and six in the book.

STORY PASSAGE

Ethan broke in before Lauren could respond, "He was going back to town to make plans to take us to Blooming Glen, where there are a lot of knight protectors, and the light is safe. Just like my dream."

Oh no! Ethan, why couldn't you keep quiet? Lauren just knew they were sunk now.

"Well, I don't know about all this other stuff yer saying." Uncle reached into his cloak and pulled out a scroll with a seal on it. "But yer pa said that if anything ever happened to him and yer ma, you should come live with Gran in Fairfields."

We just had this conversation. Lauren let out a deep sigh. Uncle didn't seem to really be listening to them, so she didn't think she should bother until the Knight Protector returned. She took the scroll. It was identical to the one the bishop had shown her in the church.

"You kids should be with kin, not all locked up in some garrison somewhere." Uncle rested his axe on the ground, balanced by both hands holding the center of the bit. "That's what yer pa would want. Time's a-wasting; let's get on packing up."

HAVE YOU EVER FELT LED BY THE HOLY SPIRIT TO GO IN A
DIFFERENT DIRECTION THAN THOSE AROUND YOU?

PASSAGE QUESTIONS

Read the STORY PASSAGE and answer the following questions in your reading journal.

1. Whose return did the kids want to wait for?
2. Where did the person they were waiting on go?
3. Where does Uncle believe the kids should go?
4. Why does Uncle think that is the best place?

Joke of the Day

What did the sketchbook say to the novel?

I'm drawing a blank.

DAY FOUR

MEMORY VERSE, VOCABULARY & READING

In your reading journal, copy this week's memory verse and draw a picture definition for each vocabulary word. Then, read chapters seven and eight in the book.

STORY PASSAGE

Lauren continued, "Uncle said he's going to take us to grandma's house."

The elder warrior dropped the reins. "Your father's brother is here?" He scanned the yard. "Where is he?"

Aiden dashed over and scooped up the reins. "He's with Ethan at the creek right now, trying to catch Sparkle Frog."

Knight Protector put his hands on his hips and scanned the woods. "After our discussion this morning, do you think he's right to do this?"

Aiden was taken aback by this. He did agree that it seemed like the still small voice was telling them to go to Blooming Glen. Knight Protector was a stranger though, and Uncle was family.

"Well, he talked to Daddy and has his paper." The quiver in Aiden's voice gave away his uncertainty. "I don't know if he heard the small voice."

"I see." Knight Protector frowned. "And you, Lauren?"

"I believe Ethan's dream and your story about Daddy changing his mind. I'm worried about the consequences if we don't follow that."

WHAT CAN YOU DO IF YOU DISAGREE WITH THOSE IN CHARGE?

PASSAGE QUESTIONS

Read the STORY PASSAGE and answer the following questions in your reading journal.

1. Where do the children believe the still small voice is urging them to go?
2. Do the children believe Uncle heard the small voice?
3. Which sentence supports the previous answer?

Joke of the Day

Did you hear about the pen that can writer underwater?
It can write other words as well.

DAY FIVE

READING & MEMORY VERSE

Read chapter nine in the book. Then, recite this week's memory verse aloud and complete the activity below. Include the coloring page and vocabulary puzzle with today's activities.

ACTIVITY: AGED PAPER

MATERIALS

- A sheet of paper
- A ball-point pen or fine-point permanent
- Coffee
- Wax paper (or similar)
- Shallow container (large enough to submerge the sheet paper in coffee)

INSTRUCTIONS

Write this week's memory verse on a sheet of a paper (or another verse of your choosing). If desired, tear the edges of the paper for added effect. Place the paper in the container.

Next, brew a cup of coffee (cold leftover coffee also works) and fill the container with enough coffee to submerge paper. Let it sit for ten to twenty minutes (longer will produce a darker color).

Then, remove the paper and lay it on the wax paper overnight to dry.

WHY DOES SOAKING THE PAPER LONGER PRODUCE A DARKER COLOR? HOW CAN WE APPLY THE SAME CONCEPT TO OUR WALK WITH GOD?

WEEK TWO
THE LOST

Memory Verse:
*"Now Samuel did not yet know the Lord, neither was the word
of the Lord yet revealed unto him."*
—1 Samuel 3:7 KJV

LAUREN

VOCABULARY

WORD LIST

As part of your daily work this week, you'll need to use a dictionary and a thesaurus to look up definitions, synonyms, and antonyms for the words below.

DRAMA   ORNATE   TALON
MALLET   POUNCE   UNISON

WORD SCRAMBLE

Rearrange each group of letters below to unscramble the words.

ATENOR

__ __ __ __ __ __

ALETML

__ __ __ __ __ __

ONUISN

__ __ __ __ __ __

UNOPEC

__ __ __ __ __ __

ALTNO

__ __ __ __ __

ARADM

__ __ __ __ __

DAY ONE

MEMORY VERSE, VOCABULARY & READING

In your reading journal, copy this week's memory verse and vocabulary definitions. Then, read chapters ten and eleven in the book.

STORY PASSAGE

Blood, water, what? Lauren felt he had completely lost it. She looked to the boys who shrugged. She did likewise. "Um… I guess that's right, but it's just gross."

Uncle did a double take. "Never mind that. What I'm saying is, family is the most important thing."

"Oh, I get it." Aiden raised his hand like he was in Sunday school. "Blood, like blood relations. But what's the water?"

"The water… it's a sayin': blood is thicker 'n' water." Uncle looked around the room for a minute like he was trying to find some example.

He shook his head. "We're kin, you see, and kin's got to stick together. So, you all need to stick with me, got it?" He put his hands on his hips. "I don't know what yer Knight Protector's plannin', but I do know yer gran would never forgive me if I let anything happen to you nibbles." He pointed at each of the children for emphasis, and then back at himself. "So, you need to follow my lead regardless of what kind of story the Knight Protector might be telling."

"OK, Coo Coo." Ethan looked at Aiden, then Lauren.

HOW CAN WE HANDLE DISAGREEMENTS IN A GODLY MANNER?

PASSAGE QUESTIONS

Read the STORY PASSAGE and answer the following questions in your reading journal.

1. What does Uncle mean by "blood is thicker 'n' water"?
2. How does Uncle feel about the Knight Protector's plan?
3. What evidence in the passage supports the previous answer?

Joke of the Day

Did you hear about the book on antigravity?
It's impossible to put down.

DAY TWO

MEMORY VERSE, VOCABULARY & READING

In your reading journal, copy this week's memory verse and list three synonyms for each vocabulary word. Then, read chapters twelve and thirteen in the book.

STORY PASSAGE

The parson stepped to Ethan's side and slowly knelt on one knee. "Please, young Ethan, tell us about Sir Nicolas."

Ethan looked at the crowd and paused for a moment, not sure where to begin. Then he pointed toward their home. "Nicolas saved Sparkle Frog from the black water." Then he pointed at his siblings. "Then, he saved Sissy and Aiden from the bad dogs."

Ethan turned to Parson with a pleading look in his eyes. "He was my friend, and I miss him. Parson, please pray, and God will make him all better."

Parson's face fell at this request, leaving a lump in Ethan's stomach.

Ethan pleaded with his hands clasped together. "I prayed, and that wasn't good enough. You pray, and he will be all better."

"Oh child," the pastor pulled Ethan to him in a kind embrace. "I am so sorry. I know you and your brother and sister have prayed much over Nicolas." Ethan began to sob into Parson's shirt. The parson stroked Ethan's hair. "God has him home in heaven now to watch over us. His mission here on Earth is done, and he is now free of all the conflict and pain that still visits these lands."

WHAT DOES THE BIBLE SAY ABOUT HEAVEN?

PASSAGE QUESTIONS

Read the STORY PASSAGE and answer the following questions in your reading journal.

1. What happened to Sir Nicolas?
2. What did Ethan pray for?
3. What evidence in the passage supports the previous answer?
4. What did Parson say happened to Sir Nicolas?

Joke of the Day

Did you know I had plans to write a book about sinkholes?
Yeah, but they fell through.

DAY THREE

MEMORY VERSE, VOCABULARY & READING

In your reading journal, copy this week's memory verse and list three antonyms for each vocabulary word. Then, read chapters fourteen and fifteen in the book.

STORY PASSAGE

"Kids, we're leavin' for grandma's house. Now!" Uncle called over his shoulder.

Lauren's mouth dropped. She didn't even get a chance to make her case. *They were really going to grandma's house, even though the still small voice told them to go to Blooming Glen. How could she explain?*

"Uncle, wait," she said.

"Daylight's a burnin', little one. We need to get on down the road." The hard look on his face made it clear he wasn't going to listen.

This made her angry, and she was about to push the issue. Then, she realized that Uncle really didn't follow the Light, so anything she added right now would be met with skepticism. Grandma followed the Light though. Grandma was very wise, and she listened to the children. *Maybe Grandma can help us avoid the consequences.*

"Boys, I'm going to use my still small voice now." She hoped the boys would pick up on what she was trying to say. She climbed into the wagon and spoke to Aidan and Ethan quietly. "We need to go with Uncle to grandma's house. Grandma can help us with Mama and Daddy, I know it."

WHAT CAN YOU DO WHEN A SITUATION IS OUT OF YOUR CONTROL?

PASSAGE QUESTIONS

Read the STORY PASSAGE and answer the following questions in your reading journal.

1. Why was Lauren angry?
2. How did she deal with the situation that was making her angry?
3. Why does Lauren think there will be consequences?
4. How does Lauren hope to avoid the consequences?

Joke of the Day

My mom used to sprinkle my pillow with sugar.
She wanted me to have sweet dreams!

DAY FOUR

MEMORY VERSE, VOCABULARY & READING

In your reading journal, copy this week's memory verse and draw a picture definition for each vocabulary word. Then, read chapters sixteen and seventeen in the book.

STORY PASSAGE

Ethan watched as Aiden tied the falconer's cord to Daddy Duck's leg and his own wrist. As soon as he removed the hood, Daddy Duck took to the sky and jerked Aiden's arm up with him. Aiden wobbled like he was going to fall off the wagon, but then grabbed the wagon's side rail and steadied himself.

Ethan laughed at the wild display. After a couple of minutes of furiously trying to escape, Daddy Duck settled down and landed on the wagon seat. Then he let out an accusatory quack at Aiden, letting the boy know he was not happy with the current situation.

Before Aiden could respond, Daddy Duck noticed the worms on the seat. The frustrated duck let out another quack at Aiden and then picked up a worm in its bill and swallowed it. Then, the duck nestled down on the seat and gobbled up another worm, keeping an eye on Aiden.

"Hate to say I told you so, but a duck ain't no falcon," Uncle called up gruffly from where he had taken a knee to stoke the fire.

"He's just getting used to the idea."

HOW DOES UNBELIEF LIMIT US?

PASSAGE QUESTIONS

Read the STORY PASSAGE and answer the following questions in your reading journal.

1. What did Daddy Duck do when Aiden removed the hood from the duck's head?
2. What affect did his actions have on Aiden?
3. How did Ethan react to the situation?
4. Who said Daddy Duck was "getting used to the idea"?
5. Why did the person say that?

Joke of the Day

I fell asleep on a crossword the other day.

I woke up with a puzzled look.

DAY FIVE

READING & MEMORY VERSE

Read chapter eighteen in the book. Then, recite this week's memory verse aloud and complete the activity below. Include the coloring page and vocabulary puzzle with today's activities.

ACTIVITY: INVISIBLE INK

MATERIALS

- Porous paper (like construction paper)
- Q-tip
- Lemon juice
- Small dish to hold the lemon juice
- Clothing iron

INSTRUCTIONS

Pour lemon juice into the small dish. Dip one end of the q-tip into the lemon juice and use it to write a message on the paper. Make sure the lemon juice saturates the paper well. Allow it to dry completely. Then, use a clothing iron set on high to apply heat to the paper on the side the message was written. Let the iron sit in place for about 30 seconds or so.

If you have any trouble revealing the message, check to make sure the lemon juice thoroughly saturated the paper and the heat was applied directly to the side on which the message was written. (Milk can be used as a substitute for lemon juice, but it doesn't work as well.)

HOW CAN WE REVEAL THE WORD OF THE LORD TO OTHERS?

WEEK THREE
IN THE BELLY

Memory Verse:
"Now the Lord had prepared a great fish to swallow up Jonah. And Jonah was in the belly of the fish three days and three nights."
—Jonah 1:17 KJV

ETHAN

VOCABULARY

WORD LIST

As part of your daily work this week, you'll need to use a dictionary and a thesaurus to look up definitions, synonyms, and antonyms for the words below.

BURR	HAUNCH	SPLAY
DIMINUTIVE	REFLEXIVE	TONIC

MAZE

Help the kids escape! Trace a path from the center of the maze to the outside.

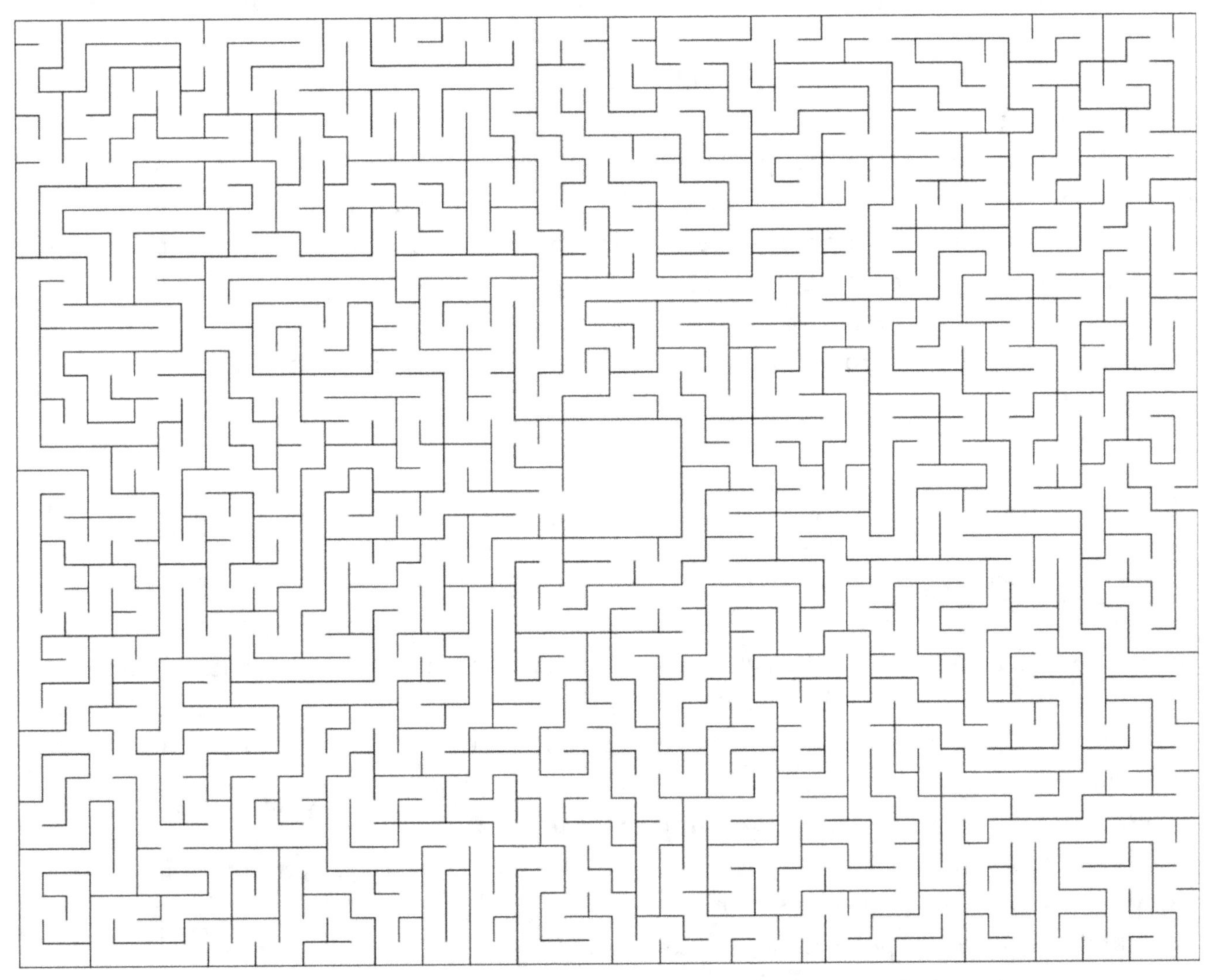

DAY ONE

MEMORY VERSE, VOCABULARY & READING

In your reading journal, copy this week's memory verse and vocabulary definitions. Then, read chapters ninteen and twenty in the book.

STORY PASSAGE

Lauren set her empty tin cup down and asked Ethan, "What are you thankful for?"

Ethan ran over and hugged Uncle. "I'm thankful for Uncle helping bring Sparkle Frog."

Uncle seemed to squirm under the hug, and his big eyes almost looked panicked by Ethan's sudden burst of emotion. He set down his cup and patted Ethan on the head. It surprised Lauren that Ethan was so affectionate after Uncle's treatment of Aiden the day before.

Aiden nodded his head. "I'm thankful Uncle helped bring Daddy Duck and that he teaches us stuff."

Lauren was not all that happy with Uncle's teaching methods. He could have helped Aiden with the duck the day before to keep him safe. She could feel heat in her cheeks, so she took a moment to compose herself. Then she picked up her kitten and petted him. "I'm thankful that Uncle let me bring Meow Meow."

Ethan let go of Uncle and stepped back, "What are you thankful for Uncle?"

Uncle raised his eyebrows and sat there slack jawed for a moment. "What? Why are you asking me?"

WHAT BLESSINGS ARE YOU THANKFUL FOR?

PASSAGE QUESTIONS

Read the STORY PASSAGE and answer the following questions in your reading journal.

1. How did Uncle feel about Ethan's words and embrace?
2. What evidence in the passage supports the previous answer?
3. Why was Lauren angry with Uncle?
4. Which sentence supports the previous answer?
5. What was Lauren thankful for?

Joke of the Day

My kids always have a tough time taking a nap, but I don't get it. I can do it with my closed.

DAY TWO

MEMORY VERSE, VOCABULARY & READING

In your reading journal, copy this week's memory verse and list three synonyms for each vocabulary word. Then, read chapters twenty-one and twenty-two in the book.

STORY PASSAGE

Uncle stepped up to them and put the head of the double-bitted axe on the ground while he leaned on the handle. "Ain't no critter here in these parts that Ol' Faithful can't get the better of. Next time I tell you to go hide, I mean go hide. I can't fight well if I have to worry about you coming up to try to help. Got it?"

"Yes, sir," Lauren replied sheepishly, and the boys just nodded.

Uncle pointed at them. "Now put those things away and get back to bed." "Yes, sir," they all responded despondently.

The boys put their arms away and followed Lauren down from the wagon, while Uncle walked to the fire. He added small branches to it and stoked it up considerably. Uncle dragged the cougar's carcass closer to the flames and began to skin it.

In the lean-to, Aiden whispered, "Sissy, why didn't you tell Uncle about the spear? It looked like you knocked the cougar out before he flipped it over and killed it."

"Yeah, Sissy? Why let Coo Coo take all the credit?" Ethan whispered.

How could she explain this to the boys? *God, you gave us these gifts, why don't people believe?*

HOW CAN WE DISCERN THE TRUTH?

PASSAGE QUESTIONS

Read the STORY PASSAGE and answer the following questions in your reading journal.

1. Why was Uncle upset?
2. What did Uncle want the children to do?
3. What happened to the cougar?
4. Why did the boys think Uncle shouldn't get all the credit for what happened to the cougar?
5. Why did Uncle not see Lauren's actions with the spear?

Joke of the Day

You know a few weeks back I spent all day writing a book about mazes. Yeah, I got lost in it.

DAY THREE

MEMORY VERSE, VOCABULARY & READING

In your reading journal, copy this week's memory verse and list three antonyms for each vocabulary word. Then, read chapters twenty-three and twenty-four in the book.

STORY PASSAGE

The daughter sat at a table with her mother's arm around her shoulder. "The night the censers exploded, there was chaos in the camp. I really don't remember how I got shuffled out of town—only that at one point, a giant threw me over his shoulder and carried me across a stream."

The matron's eyes flew wide as her mouth gaped open. "A Heath Warden, in league with the Darkness? If the giants have turned, these are truly dark days."

The acolyte was disturbed by this discussion. The censers brought the true light. With them destroyed, of course, bad things were bound to happen. He wanted to confront this heresy once and for all but decided it could wait for the rest of the story to be told.

He stood there for a moment, expecting her to continue. But the matron looked up. "Go on now, start getting ready for the lunch rush."

I need to know what happened.

The matron's upraised eyebrows and pursed lips showed him it was time to move along.

SHARE A TIME WHEN SOMETHING WAS NOT AS IT SEEMED.

PASSAGE QUESTIONS

Read the STORY PASSAGE and answer the following questions in your reading journal.

1. Who are the Heath Wardens?
2. Why is the acolyte disturbed by the discussion?
3. Does the acolyte follow the light or the darkness?
4. Was the acolyte eavesdropping?
5. Which sentence supports the previous answer?

DAY FOUR

MEMORY VERSE, VOCABULARY & READING

In your reading journal, copy this week's memory verse and draw a picture definition for each vocabulary word. Then, read chapters twenty-five and twenty-six in the book.

STORY PASSAGE

Just then, a girl in a white robe like the boy servant came out of a side room. Her hair was wet and combed straight with a part down the middle, but she had scratches on her face and arms. *Oh, that looks owie. Maybe Sparkle Frog can help.* She scurried across the room and into the kitchen.

The matron turned back to Uncle. "My daughter will be speaking at church this evening and will tell you exactly what this has to do with ale."

Uncle investigated his empty mug. "I ain't exactly the goodness and light church type, ma'am."

"Maybe you should be," the matron retorted. "If more men sought the true Light, maybe this wouldn't have happened to my daughter."

Ethan hopped up and pulled on the matron's skirt. "She looks owie. Sparkle Frog makes head eggs go away." He patted the top of his head.

She looked down at Ethan with a broad smile on her face. "That's good to know, little one. But I'll take care of my own kin. Now you all eat your vittles, and when you're done, you'll get a bath and clean clothes."

TAKE A MOMENT TO PRAY FOR THE LOST.

PASSAGE QUESTIONS

Read the STORY PASSAGE and answer the following questions in your reading journal.

1. Why does Ethan think Sparkle Frog can help the girl?
2. Which sentence supports the previous answer?
3. What does the matron believe might have prevented the girl's attack?
4. Who is the matron referring to when she said "my own kin"?

Joke of the Day

How do we know Peter was a rich fisherman?

By his net income.

DAY FIVE

READING & MEMORY VERSE

Read chapter twenty-seven in the book. Then, recite this week's memory verse aloud and complete the activity below. Include the coloring page and vocabulary puzzle with today's activities.

ACTIVITY: BIRD FEEDER

MATERIALS

- Empty milk jug
- Stick or wood dowel, 8-12"
- String, 12-18"
- Birdseed, 2-3 cups
- Scissors
- Hot glue or outdoor Modge Podge
- Paints and markers, for decorating

INSTRUCTIONS

Wash and dry the empty milk jug. Use scissors to cut two openings on the sides opposite from the handle. The jug will need to hold birdseed in the bottom, so leave at least two inches from the edge on both sides of the opening and at least three inches from the bottom.

Poke two small holes near the lid on top and two slightly larger holes in the corner beneath the openings. Push the stick through the two holes near the bottom of the jug and hot glue it into place. (This will be a perch for the birds.) Next, thread the string through the two small holes on top—but don't tie it yet. This string will be used to hang the bird feeder. Once you've selected the right spot, you'll tie it then.

Decorate the outside of the jug as desired. After it dries, fill it with bird seed and hang it outside. (Tip: Mix red pepper flakes into the bird seed to deter squirrels. It doesn't bother birds. They can't taste it, but squirrels can.)

WEEK FOUR
HOLY SPIRIT

Memory Verse:
"Now we have received, not the spirit of the world, but the spirit which is of God; that we might know the things that are freely given to us of God."
1 Corinthians 2:12 KJV

VOCABULARY

WORD LIST

As part of your daily work this week, you'll need to use a dictionary and a thesaurus to look up definitions, synonyms, and antonyms for the words below.

BUGLE   HOLLER   TALL TALE
EPILOGUE   LEGEND   VERANDA

WORD SEARCH

Find and circle the hidden vocabulary words in the puzzle below. Words may appear up, down, forwards, backwards, or diagonally.

BUGLE	HAUNCH	ORNATE	SPLAY
BURR	HOLLER	PANTOMIME	TALL TALE
CRESCENDO	LACQUER	POUNCE	TALON
DRAMA	LEGEND	PROLOGUE	TONIC
DIMINUTIVE	MALLET	REFLEXIVE	UNISON
EPILOGUE	METAPHOR	SILHOUETTE	VERANDA

```
U N I S O N V S P L A Y R P R O L O G U E G I C Y
I S W D N L A C Q U E R F L K L F F H N Y I O W L
S T C T I B U G L E I T T P P Y E F D Q L A Z P C
G A H R C M V M A L L E T X L V T P Q R Z T Z D S
H L T G E R I Z L W R R M M H F B K I N A B L V K
R L G D K S E N G S I L H O U E T T E L U M U H I
Z T Z Y P L C F U E R O H O L L E R Y Y O Z A G X
H A T Z O M E E L T G M Z L D G X B U D H G G R Z
A L O J U E S G N E I P V R Z L Q G U O U H U R P
U E N C N T X B E D X V P A N T O M I M E N X E V
N I I R C A A U C N O I E I T V L I O R N A T E N
C I C Y E P C R M D D K V T H A G V E R A N D A E
H B E Z F H E R D J E Q T E Q K L Q X C F W Y A F
H E W A M O L A V C M I Q M Q W X O D I S F A K V
F Z I O Q R R P M M V X K P H A W L N N H N T V J
```

DAY ONE

MEMORY VERSE, VOCABULARY & READING

In your reading journal, copy this week's memory verse and vocabulary definitions. Then, read chapters twenty-eight and twenty-nine in the book.

STORY PASSAGE

"Save Bear!" Tok cried as he held his hand folded before him. "Pweeze"

"But Uncle said he didn't think we could do a scout without being seen." Aiden edged toward the hole in the barn.

"No, Uncle was worried about if we didn't have a guide we'd get caught." She pointed her spear at Tok. "We have a guide. I think he'll go on a scout with us."

Aiden shook his head. "Tok says the place is nearby. We can be sneaky. If it looks too dangerous, we can come get Uncle. If we ask for his help, he might just keep us locked up here, and poor Tok won't be able to get his bear."

"Yeah, Uncle never believes us, Sissy." Ethan jutted out his chin. "You beat that cougar, and he said he did."

Lauren slowly lowered her spear, shaking her head. "He told us he wouldn't even take us to spy things out. It feels dishonest to just go without telling him."

Tok's eyes filled with tears. *Would the girl not help now? She had to help!* "Save Bear?"

Ethan ran up and hugged Tok. This made him feel better, maybe the little one would help him.

HAVE YOU EVER BEEN ASKED TO HELP, BUT FELT YOU COULDN'T?

PASSAGE QUESTIONS

Read the STORY PASSAGE and answer the following questions in your reading journal.

1. Where are the kids?
2. Who asks the kids for help?
3. What does the person ask the kids to do?
4. Why are the kids uncertain about helping?
5. How does Tok react to the situation?

DAY TWO

MEMORY VERSE, VOCABULARY & READING

In your reading journal, copy this week's memory verse and list three synonyms for each vocabulary word. Then, read chapters thirty and thirty-one in the book.

STORY PASSAGE

Ethan jumped up. "Yeah, like last night. Tok needed help, and we saved the Bear and broke the bad men's tent."

"You did what?" Uncle exclaimed, his eyes getting a wild look. Red rushed into his face.

No! Ethan, why'd you open your mouth? This is going to be a mess. Lauren attempted to diffuse the situation. "The creature we told you about was a Bjorn Born. The dark ones had captured his bear, and he needed help freeing it. Our weapons activated, so we knew we needed to help."

Uncle stood up, clenched his fists, and began to pace, looking at Lauren with clear anger in his eyes. "When I saw the mud on the hem of the boys' pants and a couple briars on yer skirt, I chalked it up to being in a dirty stable. But now you're telling me you left the stable and didn't tell me? What did I tell you kids about blood being thicker'n water?"

The hurt look on his face made the children feel ashamed of themselves. Uncle went over and picked up the Good Book.

"Yer pa was always Good Book this and that. It's clear that's all gone to yer heads."

WHAT ARE SOME COMMON MISCONCEPTIONS ABOUT THE BIBLE?

PASSAGE QUESTIONS

Read the STORY PASSAGE and answer the following questions in your reading journal.

1. Why did Uncle get angry?
2. How did Lauren feel about Ethan telling Uncle that they saved Bear?
3. What evidence in the passage supports the previous answer?

DAY THREE

MEMORY VERSE, VOCABULARY & READING

In your reading journal, copy this week's memory verse and list three antonyms for each vocabulary word. Then, read chapters thirty-two and thirty-three in the book.

STORY PASSAGE

"Uncle, we can beat him." Ethan branded his shield in the air.

Uncle paused. *Could they really do it?* Lauren's spear strikes had been dead on every time. Only the Light could give a little boy the power to cut clean through an axe.

Uncle looked back down the bridge; the giant had already cleared half of it. Now that he was closer, Uncle could see it was wearing some kind of harness and had some black iron contraption on his back that was spewing black smoke into the air. *I don't know what that is, but it can't be good.* He realized he was till holding the writ in an iron grip and shoved it into his waist pouch. Then tossed the torch where he thought it might best light the battle and pulled Ol' faithful off his back.

"Lauren, when he gets close enough, try yer spear." Uncle felt a tingle go up his spine and down his right arm. He looked at his hand and it seemed like Ol' Faithful had taken on the blue glow of Ethan's shield.

Must be seein' things, He shook his head and turned back to the advancing giant.

"Is that three little children playing warrior I see?" the giant bellowed as he strode across the bridge.

HOW DO WE BATTLE EVIL FORCES IN OUR WORLD?

PASSAGE QUESTIONS

Read the STORY PASSAGE and answer the following questions in your reading journal.

1. Who are Uncle and the children fighting?
2. What is spewing black smoke into the air?
3. Why does Uncle's axe seem to take on a blue glow like the children's weapons?

Joke of the Day

What do you get when you cross a pig with a centipede.

Bacon and legs.

DAY FOUR

MEMORY VERSE, VOCABULARY & READING

In your reading journal, copy this week's memory verse and draw a picture definition for each vocabulary word. Then, read chapters thirty-four and thirty-five in the book.

STORY PASSAGE

The geese landed gracefully in the dawn light. One on either side of the waterlogged figure floating on driftwood in the Awoi river. Their platinum feathers reflected the light all around them, making the area as bright as noonday. Each goose swam to a shoulder and ducked its head under an arm. They lifted their heads and pulled the big frontiersman up off the driftwood.

They floated with him down the river where it met the great Muddy River and on to Francis Ford. There they slowly waddled up onto the shore, with their charge in tow. Once he was out of the water, they put their heads down and walked back out from under his arms. Then, the geese patiently waited.

As the sun reached noon, the man's eyes opened. He slowly sat up on his elbows, and his eyes were dazzled by the glorious light reflected from the geese. A wave of peace and healing flowed over the man. "I'm still drawin' breath, so ain't no giant gonna hurt my nibbles."

HOW DOES SALVATION CHANGE US?

PASSAGE QUESTIONS

Read the STORY PASSAGE and answer the following questions in your reading journal.

1. Which river was the frontiersman floating on?
2. What time of day did he make it to shore?
3. How did he make it to shore?
4. When did the frontiersman finally open his eyes?

Joke of the Day

Why did the omelet flunk out of school?

It failed its eggs-zams.

DAY FIVE

READING & MEMORY VERSE

Read chapter thirty-six in the book. Then, recite this week's memory verse aloud and complete the activity below. Include the coloring page and vocabulary puzzle with today's activities.

ACTIVITY: 3D GLASSES

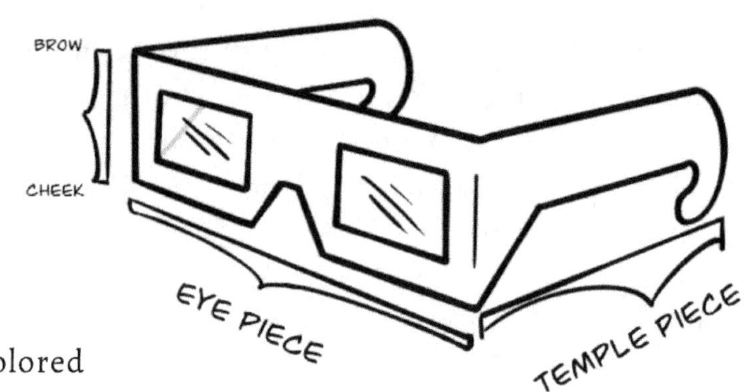

MATERIALS

- Glue or tape
- Ruler and scissors
- Red and blue markers
- Card stock or manilla folder
- Blue and red cellophane (clear, colored plastic binder dividers will work)

INSTRUCTIONS

First, measure from just behind your ear to you brow for the temple pieces. Then, measure across the face and from brow to cheek for the eye piece. Use these measurements to draw a template of your glasses onto a piece of card stock.

Next, cut out your glasses, including holes for the eyes. (Avoid cutting the glasses into multiple pieces. It works best if the glass frame is cut as one piece.) Decorate as desired.

The frame of your glasses can act as a guide to measure and cut out the lens. Cut at least one red and one blue lens from the clear, colored cellophane. (Adding a second or third layer of the cellophane to each lens can intensify the 3-D effect, so long as the layers aren't too thick to see through.) Glue or tape the lens into place.

Once your glasses are assembled, create a 3-D image by holding the red and blue markers together while drawing. Then, use your glasses to view it.

HOW DO WE DISCERN WHAT IS GOOD FROM WHAT ONLY LOOKS GOOD?

FEAR
NO
EVIL

WEEK ONE
SEPARATED

Memory Verse:
"Yea, though I walk through the valley of the shadow of death, I will fear no evil: for thou [art] with me; thy rod and thy staff they comfort me."
— Psalms 23:4 KJV

AIDEN

VOCABULARY

WORD LIST

As part of your daily work this week, you'll need to use a dictionary and a thesaurus to look up definitions, synonyms, and antonyms for the words below.

ABOMINATION   CLAMBERED   RUDDER
BANISHED   RITE   SPYGLASS

SECRET MESSAGE

This week's vocabulary words have been used to form the message below, but it's been encrypted to keep it a secret. Determine which letter in the alphabet corresponds to each number to decode the message.

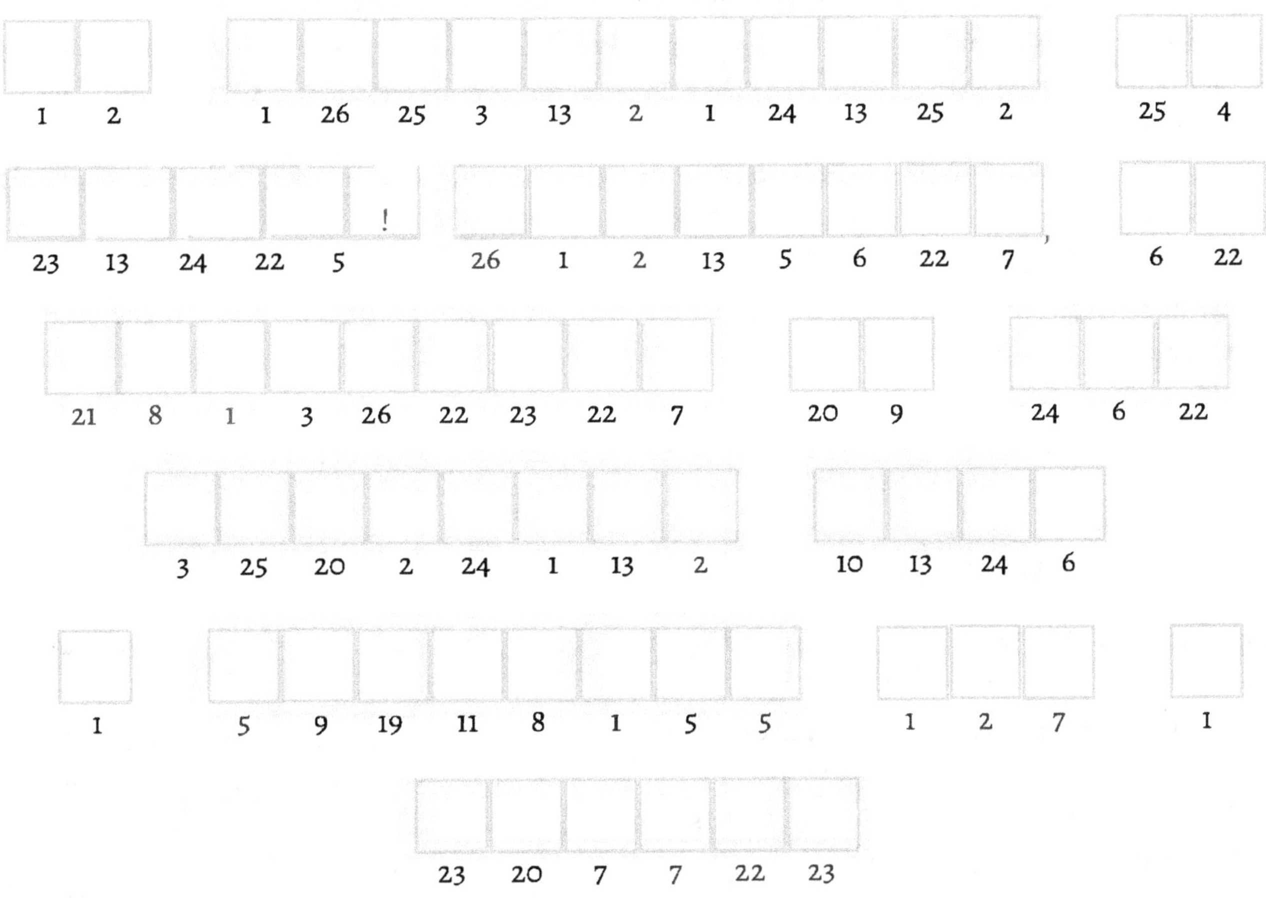

DAY ONE

MEMORY VERSE, VOCABULARY & READING

In your reading journal, copy this week's memory verse and vocabulary definitions. Then, read chapters one and two in the book.

STORY PASSAGE

Lauren's voice was strong as she read. "The Lord is my shepherd; I shall not want. He maketh me to lie down in green pastures: he leadeth me beside the still waters. He restoreth my soul: he leadeth me in the paths of righteousness for his name's sake. Yea, though I walk through the valley of the shadow of death, I will fear no evil."

A yell from outside interrupted Lauren's reading. "GIANT!"

The peace Aiden found evaporated as his heart leapt into his throat. "Oh, no! He found us!"

Aiden scrambled out of his chair, pulling his doffed sword belt along with him. *If that's the same Giant, then he defeated Uncle at the bridge.* Aiden choked back his sorrow and focused on buckling his sword belt.

Lauren and Ethan began to follow Aiden's example, but Knight Protector's strong voice halted them, "Wait children! What did that verse just say?"

Aiden paused and his brow crinkled. "Fear no evil?"

"That's right, children. The good Lord has delivered you from the valley of the shadow to our care.

WHAT FEARS DO YOU PRAY ABOUT?

PASSAGE QUESTIONS

Read the STORY PASSAGE and answer the following questions in your reading journal.

1. What does the verse that Lauren is reading mean by "The Lord is my shepherd?"
2. Did Aiden's heart really "leap into his throat?" What does that saying mean?
3. What is Uncle trying to say to the children in the last sentence of the story passage?

Joke of the Day

When does it rain money?
When there is change in the weather!

DAY TWO

MEMORY VERSE, VOCABULARY & READING

In your reading journal, copy this week's memory verse and list three synonyms for each vocabulary word. Then, read chapter three in the book.

STORY PASSAGE

"Lauren! I'm going to get Aiden." Knight Protector's voice rang from the opposite side of the wagon over the din of flopping fish and yells. "Get rope from the wagon."

Her resolved faltered, and she laid there blankly staring under the wagon at Knight Protectors boots. She was drained, like she'd been running a race for days. "I… I can't," Lauren feebly replied.

The sound of clanking metal on the other side of the wagon drowned out her voice. Knight Protector's chest piece hit the floor, and his feet appeared to leap up and out of view. She heard a big splash and assumed the old warrior was going after Aiden.

Lauren lay there for what seemed an eternity. Yells and splashing filling the night. She knew every minute counted to save Aiden, but her limbs were frozen in place.

"Lauren, I have him." Knight Protector's voice was muted, but she could hear a hint of desperation.

God, I just can't do this. The carp are going to knock me in the water too. Please help.

TELL ABOUT A TIME WHEN YOU WERE SCARED AND FELT "FROZEN."

PASSAGE QUESTIONS

Read the STORY PASSAGE and answer the following questions in your reading journal.

1. What does Lauren's "resolve faltered" mean?
2. Give some examples of how Lauren is feeling in the moment.
3. What is Lauren afraid of in this moment?

Joke of the Day

Why were the students' grades underwater?
They were all below C level!

DAY THREE

MEMORY VERSE, VOCABULARY & READING

In your reading journal, copy this week's memory verse and list three antonyms for each vocabulary word. Then, read chapters four and five in the book.

STORY PASSAGE

"A warden using the evil of the Iron Hills against the creatures we are sworn to protect! Unthinkable!" Tye's eyes narrowed. "La'Ren of the Tower, if I had not seen the Arcoirisana bless you, I would think you a liar."

Heat rushed to Lauren's cheeks. Before she could respond in her own defense, Sparkle Frog let out a croak.

Tye bowed in the direction of the Frog, "But I did see it, and can't think why you might choose to lie to me," she put an open hand out to Lauren. "Come, let us get you warm and dry. You can tell me your wild tale, and I can think about what to do about this abomination you speak of."

The heat drained from Lauren's cheeks, and a dull ache for her lost siblings overtook her. "OK, but I need you to promise me you'll help me look for my brothers."

PASSAGE QUESTIONS

Read the STORY PASSAGE and answer the following questions in your reading journal.

1. Why did heat rush to Lauren's cheeks?
2. Why did Tye believe Lauren's story?
3. Why did Tye use the word abomination?
4. What does Lauren ask Tye to help her do?

Joke of the Day

Why did the baker's credit card get declined?
He didn't have enough dough!

DAY FOUR

MEMORY VERSE, VOCABULARY & READING

In your reading journal, copy this week's memory verse and draw a picture definition for each vocabulary word. Then, read chapter six in the book.

STORY PASSAGE

Behind the attacker, a group of a dozen similarly tattered Bjorn-born stood blocking the exit from what used to be the back of the ferry. "Aiden! Sissy! Help! I'm surrounded!" Ethan's yell caused all of the Bjorn-born to flinch back and look all around. When help didn't come, they moved in closer, menacing Ethan with their spears.

He looked for his shield and remembered dropping it in the wagon just before the lights went out. He was alone and unarmed. Seeking divine inspiration, he looked up and realized the sky above them had the Darkness haze they saw over the parson's house. A chill went down his spine and weakened his knees.

What did the Good Book say? In the valley of the shadow, fear no evil. God had helped him defeat the hell hounds and save Tok's bear; God would save him now too. He took a deep breath, and confidence filled his chest. These guys were littler than he was by at least a head. If he could get past them, he could outrun them. Maybe if he talked to them, he could squeeze past.

HOW DOES GOD HELP GIVE YOU CONFIDENCE?

PASSAGE QUESTIONS

Read the STORY PASSAGE and answer the following questions in your reading journal.

1. What does it mean when it says the Bjorn-born were "menacing Ethan with their spears?"
2. Why did a chill go down Ethan's spine that "weakened his knees?"
3. How did Ethan regain his confidence?
4. What was Ethan's idea?

> **Joke of the Day**
>
> Why was everyone grouchy after drinking the apple cider?
> It was made from crab apples!

DAY FIVE

READING & MEMORY VERSE

Read chapter seven in the book. Then, recite this week's memory verse aloud and complete the activity below. Include the coloring page and vocabulary puzzle with today's activities.

ACTIVITY: RUDDER EXPERIMENT

MATERIALS

- Lid to a small, square, plastic container
- Small dowel rod
- Rubber band
- Large popsicle stick
- Box cutter (to be used by adult)

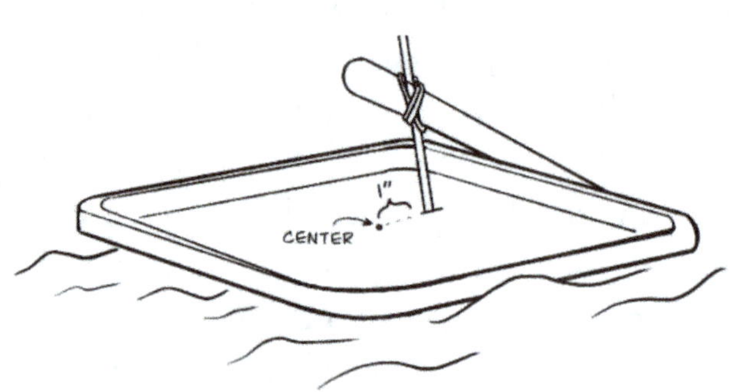

INSTRUCTIONS

An adult needs to use a box cutter to make a hole in the lid. The lid will be your raft. Make the hole about an inch away from the center, towards one of the sides. It needs to be big enough for the rod to turn, but still fit snugly so the rod doesn't fall through. Cut the dowel rod in half. Attach the popsicle stick flat against the rod with a rubber band, and pointed down at about a 45-degree angle. Then insert your rod into the hole in the lid. Now, you have a raft!

Place the raft into the water with the dowel rod up. The popsicle stick should stick into the water enough to use as a rudder. If not, adjust the rubber band and popsicle stick to get a better angle. You should be able to turn your dowel rod different ways to adjust the rudder and change the direction your raft floats.

HOW DO YOU USE GOD'S WORD TO HELP YOU STEER IN THE WORLD?

Memory Verse:

"Fear thou not; for I am with thee: be not dismayed; for I am thy God: I will strengthen thee; yea, I will help thee; yea, I will uphold thee with the right hand of my righteousness."
— Isaiah 41:10 KJV

LAUREN

VOCABULARY

WORD LIST

As part of your daily work this week, you'll need to use a dictionary and a thesaurus to look up definitions, synonyms, and antonyms for the words below.

CHARRED   GRANDEUR   RAMSHACKLE
FORAGING   FALTERED   VENGEANCE

WORD SCRAMBLE

Rearrange each group of letters below to unscramble the words.

DRAECHR

__ __ __ __ __ __ __

NAIGGOFR

__ __ __ __ __ __ __ __

ARERDGNU

__ __ __ __ __ __ __ __

ETFAELRD

__ __ __ __ __ __ __ __

CKLASMREHA

__ __ __ __ __ __ __ __ __ __

VNNEGACEE

__ __ __ __ __ __ __ __ __

DAY ONE

MEMORY VERSE, VOCABULARY & READING

In your reading journal, copy this week's memory verse and vocabulary definitions. Then, read chapter eight in the book.

STORY PASSAGE

"But my ma'ma tells me that is not our way, that we must save this creature because it knows not what it does."

"I think your mother is right," Lauren said. "After I knocked the Darkness out of Tok's bear, it let Tok get on its back and ride as if they were best of friends."

Tye put a hand on Lauren's shoulder. "La'Ren of the Tower, do you think your spear can save this bear?"

God, is this why you brought me here? A wave of power coursed through Lauren as she reached for her spear. It immediately came to life.

Tye gaped at the sight. "La'Ren of the Tower, I did not believe you. But this is true power."

"It's not my power; God gives it to me when he wants." Lauren continued, "Saving this bear must be part of his plan."

"Come. The bear will be foraging now. We should eat." Tye walked towards the fire. "Tell me more about your God while I prepare the meal."

Lauren was suddenly overwhelmed. *God how can I explain the whole Good Book over lunch?*

HAS TELLING OTHERS ABOUT GOD EVER OVERWHELMED YOU?

PASSAGE QUESTIONS

Read the STORY PASSAGE and answer the following questions in your reading journal.

1. What does Tye's ma'ma mean when she says the bear "knows not what it does?"
2. What experience does Lauren have to give to Tye that her mother is right?
3. Explain what overwhelmed means?
4. Why does Lauren feel so overwhelmed?

Joke of the Day

There's one good thing about being hit in the head with a bottle of soda. It's a soft drink!

DAY TWO

MEMORY VERSE, VOCABULARY & READING

In your reading journal, copy this week's memory verse and list three synonyms for each vocabulary word. Then, read chapter nine in the book.

STORY PASSAGE

Ethan could smell the stuff in the gourd now, and it stunk. Like when cider went bad. He definitely didn't want that. The meat reminded him of the time Father burned a rotten coon on the trash pile.

Not knowing exactly how to respond, he just said, "No, thank you."

"You eat meat, drink kefir." The warrior shook the items at him

"My Daddy wouldn't like that," Ethan pulled out a tomato from his pouch. "I have food."

"Bah! Ba'bee food!" the warrior spat and glared at Ethan. "Long trip to hoo'man camp. Need real food."

"Well, I guess I'm a baby then," spilled out of Ethan's mouth before he could think about it. *What did I just do?* His stomach clenched. *Will he make me eat their poison food?*

"Bah!" The warrior shook his head then took another drink of the awful stuff in the gourd. "Ba'bee, stay here." He pointed at a six-foot log lying on the ground.

Ethan obeyed without a word, thankful for not being forced to eat the Darkness food.

HOW CAN GOD HELP US STAND UP TO OTHERS?

PASSAGE QUESTIONS

Read the STORY PASSAGE and answer the following questions in your reading journal.

1. What is making the food bad?
2. List the ways that Ethan responds to Chief's pressure to eat the awful food.
3. Why does Chief think Ethan needs to eat the food?

Joke of the Day

What did the first sock say to the second one in the dryer?
I'll see you next time around!

DAY THREE

MEMORY VERSE, VOCABULARY & READING

In your reading journal, copy this week's memory verse and list three antonyms for each vocabulary word. Then, read chapters ten and eleven in the book.

STORY PASSAGE

"This savior, he takes your disobedience against your Elders away?" Tye was crying now.

"Yeah, that's one thing." Deep down, Lauren was still feeling guilty for just lying on the ferry's floor when Knight Protector needed help, "During the battle, my elder asked me to throw a rope."

Lauren faltered a moment as her tears began. "I was too afraid of the fish that were attacking us, and I hid instead. Knight Protector and my brother Aiden were both stunned by the giant catfish because I didn't help when I was asked."

Lauren broke down, and Tye moved to her side and put an arm around her. "I too disobeyed my elder. I was tasked to watch my brother. Instead, I left him sleeping on his own while I went to the creek for a swim. When I returned, the bear had him and was taking him into the woods. By the time I got weapons to chase her, she was gone."

They both cried over their failures to save their brothers. "The Good Book says if we believe in the Savior and confess our misdeeds, we will be forgiven."

WHAT DOES THE BIBLE SAY ABOUT FORGIVENESS?

PASSAGE QUESTIONS

Read the STORY PASSAGE and answer the following questions in your reading journal.

1. What did Lauren feel guilty about in the story passage?
2. What happened to Tye's brother?
3. What knowledge did Lauren have that reassured them?

Joke of the Day

What does Meow Meow like to eat on his birthday?
Cake and mice cream!

DAY FOUR

MEMORY VERSE, VOCABULARY & READING

In your reading journal, copy this week's memory verse and draw a picture definition for each vocabulary word. Then, read chapter twelve in the book.

STORY PASSAGE

If he was going to be the leader of the Iron Hills, he needed to take charge now. He held out the chalice in one hand and poured it back into the pool. "By my own hands, I defeated Ursa and reclaimed the Horn of Power from the outsider's temple; it will be by my own hands that I take the waters of my destiny."

The guards on either side of the pool immediately snapped their spears to his neck. The high priestess lazily held up her hand. "Hold." She sighed. "What is this, blasphemy?"

"Your Holiness, only a truly penitent man can hope to lead the people of the hills." He gingerly avoided the spears at his neck as he slowly knelt in front of the pool. Then he looked up at her. "To stand imperiously over the people as the waters make their choice would surely condemn me to dust."

The high priestess' demeanor cracked. At first her eyes went wide, then she recoiled slightly. *Gotcha.* She knew that if he drank from the pool and didn't die that her days as ruler were over. He also knew, with such a pious answer, she'd have a revolt if she didn't let him finish his way.

HOW CAN YOU TELL IF SOMEONE IS GOOD OR JUST LOOKS THAT WAY?

PASSAGE QUESTIONS

Read the STORY PASSAGE and answer the following questions in your reading journal.

1. Why won't Refi'Cul's evil plan work if he has to drink from a cup?
2. How does he trick the high priestess into letting him drink from the pool with his hands?
3. What is a penitent man?

Joke of the Day

I heard a joke about a chocolate bar,
and it wasn't very funny.
So, I just snickered!

DAY FIVE

READING & MEMORY VERSE

Read chapter thirteen in the book. Then, recite this week's memory verse aloud and complete the activity below. Include the coloring page and vocabulary puzzle with today's activities.

ACTIVITY: ORANGE SURGERY

MATERIALS

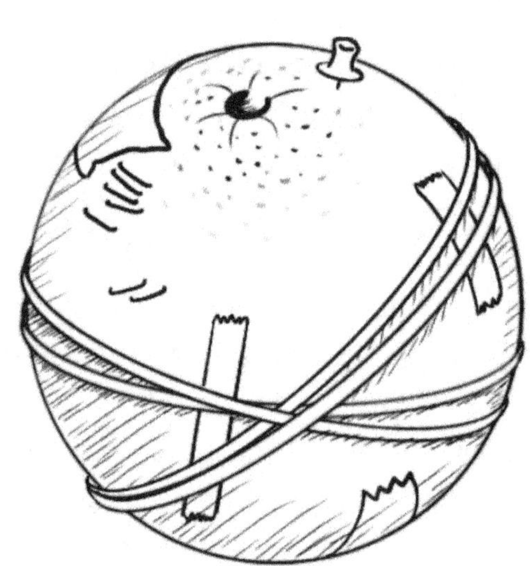

- An orange and a paper plate for each person
- An assortment of office supplies (various kinds of tape, staplers, paper clips, rubber bands, strings, glue, and anything else that might help put an orange back together)
- A timer
- Wet wipes or paper towels for cleanup

INSTRUCTIONS

Set a timer for two minutes. During which, each person will peel their oranges and pull apart the slices. Place the peels and slices in two separate piles on the plates. Then try completing the reconstruction challenge. Gather the office supplies together, placing where everyone participating can reach them, and set a timer for five minutes. Use the office supplies to put your orange back together before time runs out.

OFFICE SUPPLIES CAN ONLY BE USED ONE AT A TIME. If you are using the tape, you must return the tape before you can use another item, like the stapler. The person whose orange looks the most like it originally did at the end of five minutes wins. Pick someone not doing the challenge to be the judge.

HOW ARE THE EFFECTS OF SIN SIMILAR TO THE ORANGE? WHO CAN UNDO THE EFFECTS OF SIN IN OUR LIVES? HOW DOES HE DO THAT?

WEEK THREE
TRAPPED

Memory Verse:
"For God hath not given us the spirit of fear; but of power, and of love, and of a sound mind."
— 2 Timothy 1:7 KJV

ETHAN

VOCABULARY

WORD LIST

As part of your daily work this week, you'll need to use a dictionary and a thesaurus to look up definitions, synonyms, and antonyms for the words below.

APOTHECARY	LEAN-TO	STALACTITES
INFIRMARY	OMINOUS	TUNIC

MAZE

Help the kids find their way! Trace a path from the center of the maze to the outside.

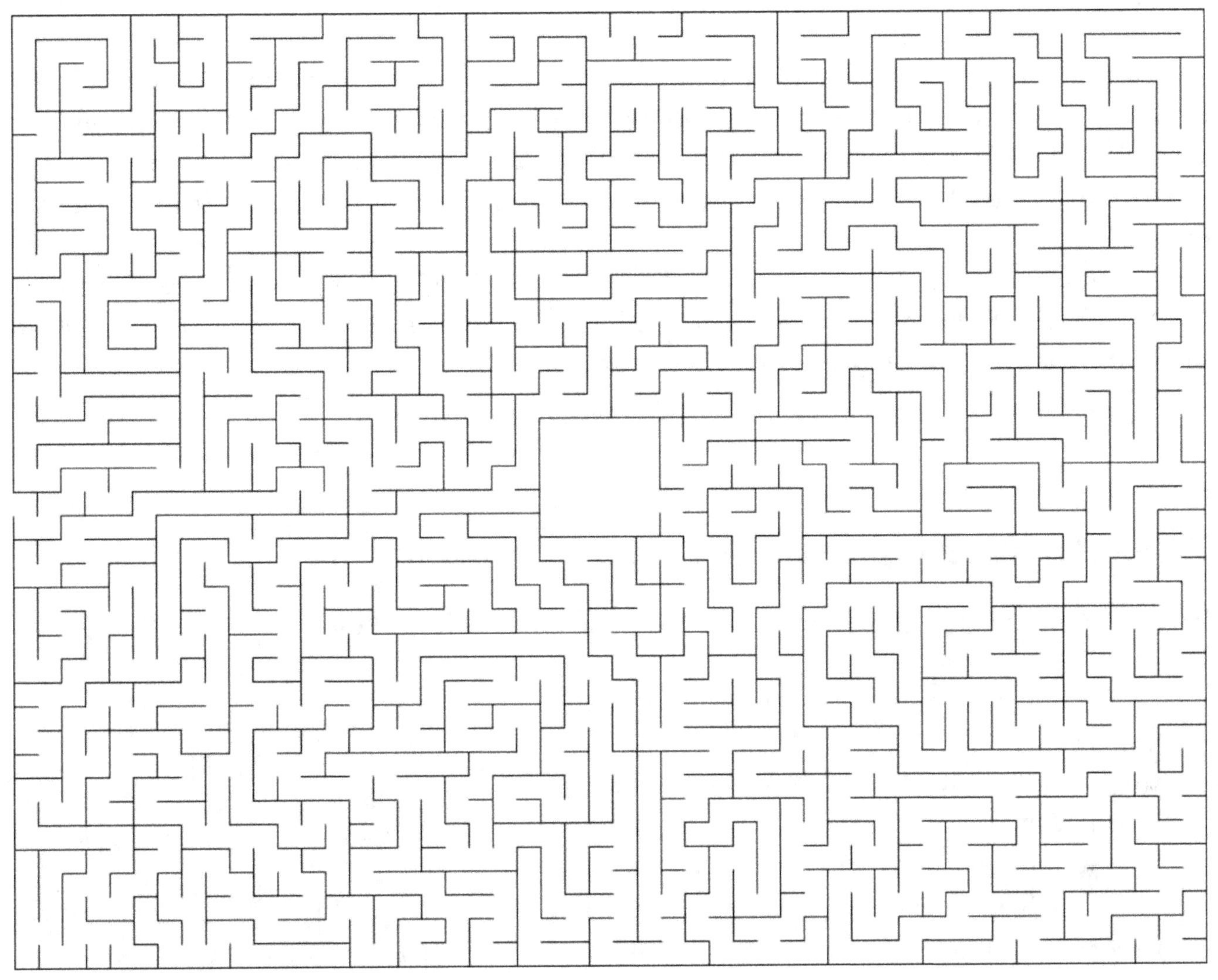

DAY ONE

MEMORY VERSE, VOCABULARY & READING

In your reading journal, copy this week's memory verse and vocabulary definitions. Then, read chapters fourteen and fifteen in the book.

STORY PASSAGE

"Hoo'man, why bear not eat you?" the creature asked as Ethan walked to Baby Bear.

"Because I shared my food with him." Ethan patted his pouch. "He likes carrots."

"Yes, yes. Share with the bear." Besta sat down on the ledge. "Before Darkness, that was way."

Baby Bear nudged the apple in Ethan's hand. He gave it to his friend but hoped it wouldn't make him sick.

"Now bears get dark." Besta hung her head. "Now bears just eat meat. Eat my babies." Ethan couldn't see in the dim flickering light, but he thought she was crying. *She must be a grandma Bjorn-born like I thought.* He frowned, and his eyes got a little watery, too.

"Chief think. Eat meat. Grow strong. Defeat bear." Besta shook her head. "That not our way."

He felt really bad for all of the good Bjorn-born. They didn't have a tower to protect them from the Darkness. Now he understood why Father wanted them to light the tower in Blooming Glen. These people needed the Light.

DO YOU KNOW OF PEOPLE THAT NEED GOD'S LIGHT?

PASSAGE QUESTIONS

Read the STORY PASSAGE and answer the following questions in your reading journal.

1. What was Ethan's answer when Besta asked him why the bear didn't eat him?
2. What did Besta say happened "before Darkness?"
3. Why was Besta sad?
4. What helped Ethan understand why they needed to light the tower in Blooming Glen?

Joke of the Day

I have a favorite mason jar that I call my "boom box."
I use it for all of my jams!

DAY TWO

MEMORY VERSE, VOCABULARY & READING

In your reading journal, copy this week's memory verse and list three synonyms for each vocabulary word. Then, read chapter sixteen in the book.

STORY PASSAGE

"You think the Darkness can stand against that?" Mother pointed to Aiden's sword.

First Sister faltered for a moment. "They took all our weapons, control hell hounds, and have blocked the light in the temple. I've seen the power your son wields, but is he alone enough?"

Mother looked at Aiden. "What do you think?"

Aiden stood there for a moment, concentrating on his breathing to clear his mind. *God, I don't know what to do. I want to save* Father, *but is that what we need to do now?* The fire on the sword went out. Aiden felt the chill of the mountains and knew the right thing to do.

He swallowed a lump in his throat. "Mama, I don't fear the evil. But I don't think that's our mission. We need to shine our light in Blooming Glen, and then save Daddy." As if to emphasize the point, the sword erupted into flame.

Mother nodded as a tear rolled down her cheek.

WHAT DO YOU DO WHEN YOU ARE FACED WITH A DIFFICULT CHOICE?

PASSAGE QUESTIONS

Read the STORY PASSAGE and answer the following questions in your reading journal.

1. How did Aiden make his decision?
2. What made his choice clear?
3. How did Mama feel about Aiden's choice?

Joke of the Day

Why does the NBA require basketball players to wear bibs at dinner?
Because they're dribblers!

DAY THREE

MEMORY VERSE, VOCABULARY & READING

In your reading journal, copy this week's memory verse and list three antonyms for each vocabulary word. Then, read chapters seventeen and eighteen in the book.

STORY PASSAGE

Ethan caught the glint of green again and then gingerly reached in to grab it. He pulled carefully and found a green jewel in his fingers attached to the hilt of a long dagger. In Ethan's small hands, it was almost a short sword. An oilcloth fell to the ground as he pulled the blade free.

Ethan's heart raced that he could break the lock on Baby Bear's cage. The light refracting through the jewel dazzled him, but the blood rolling off the back of his hand brought him back to the imminent danger around them.

He put the dagger down for a second and wrapped the oilcloth around his wounded hand, then he picked the dagger up in his right hand and the food bag in his left.

Lok looked Ethan in the eye, "We go!" the roar of the bear punctuated his urgency.

"Yes, let's go." They hurried out of the barge. Ethan was surprised to see a pile of carrots just outside the main glow of the fire. So, he stopped. "I can add a few more."

"No, food for bear," Lok grabbed Ethan's arm and pulled him. "E'tan, go fast."

HAS GOD EVER GIVEN HELP TO YOU AT JUST THE RIGHT MOMENT?

PASSAGE QUESTIONS

Read the STORY PASSAGE and answer the following questions in your reading journal.

1. What did Ethan find in the box? What did he think it would help him do?
2. Do you think the oil cloth fell out of the box by coincidence?
3. Why do you think Lok insisted on leaving the carrots for the mama bear?

Joke of the Day

What does a cheetah call an antelope that got away?
FAST-food!

DAY FOUR

MEMORY VERSE, VOCABULARY & READING

In your reading journal, copy this week's memory verse and draw a picture definition for each vocabulary word. Then, read chapter ninteen in the book.

STORY PASSAGE

"Tye! You have the Light!" Lauren cried in triumph as she finally moved the boy to face that direction. "Strike the bear now!"

The bear turned towards them, and Tye threw the spear with all she had. The holy blade struck true in the bear's chest, and a pulse of blue-green light cascaded out from that point to cover the bear in a flash of light. It flopped unconscious to the ground.

The shield's light dimmed considerably but still provided some light to the clearing. Lauren helped Tye's brother off the ground and pointed him towards the giantess.

Thunder boomed, and rain began to fall. "Tye, we should get in out of the rain. The bear won't wake up for a while, but it should be friendly now."

Tye merely nodded and scooped her brother up in her arms. She laughed as tears of joy ran down her face. "La'Ren of the Tower, you saved my brother! I can return to my people redeemed!"

Lauren shook her head, "No, Tye. You have the power of God's Light in you. The Savior redeemed you." Lauren followed the joyful siblings into the cave.

DO YOU KNOW OF A TIME WHEN THE SAVIOR
CHANGED SOMEONE'S LIFE?

PASSAGE QUESTIONS

Read the STORY PASSAGE and answer the following questions in your reading journal.

1. What happened to the bear as it turned to attack?
2. Why did Tye think Lauren saved her brother?
3. What sentence describes the emotion Tye felt when her brother was saved?

DAY FIVE

READING & MEMORY VERSE

Read chapter twenty in the book. Then, recite this week's memory verse aloud and complete the activity below. Include the coloring page and vocabulary puzzle with today's activities.

ACTIVITY: MAKE A CAVE

MATERIALS

- Playdough
- A small glass bowl
- Sugar cubes
- Warm water
- A toothpick

INSTRUCTIONS

Place a thick layer of playdough in the bottom of the bowl. Next, put sugar cubes on top of the playdough, and add a second, thin layer of playdough on top. Flatten the top layer of playdough over the sugar cubes like a roof, but don't squish it down into the cubes. Make sure the playdough roof edges are pushed against the edges of the bowl.

Poke some holes through the top layer of playdough with a toothpick, and pour water into the bowl to make it "rain." The sugar cubes will melt, leaving a cave!

The sugar cubes and playdough represent a layer of limestone rock between two layers of earth. Over a long period of time, rainwater eats away the limestone layers of rock in the earth, leaving a hollow space.

SIMILARLY, JESUS OFFERS SALVATION TO WASH AWAY OUR SINS. WHAT CAN WE DO TO FILL THE SPACE IN OUR LIVES WITH GOD'S LOVE?

WEEK FOUR
RESCUED

Memory Verse:
"I sought the LORD, and he heard me, and
delivered me from all my fears."
— Psalms 34:4

VOCABULARY

WORD LIST

As part of your daily work this week, you'll need to use a dictionary and a thesaurus to look up definitions, synonyms, and antonyms for the words below.

ANGUISH	FACETS	OVERSHADOWED
CONSOLED	HILT	PENDULUM

WORD SEARCH

Find and circle the hidden vocabulary words in the puzzle below. Words may appear up, down, forwards, backwards, or diagonally.

ABOMINATION	CONSOLED	INFIRMARY	RITE
ANGUISH	FACETS	LEAN-TO	RUDDER
APOTHECARY	FALTERED	OMINOUS	SPYGLASS
BANISHED	FORAGING	OVERSHADOWED	STALACTITES
CHARRED	GRANDEUR	PENDULUM	TUNIC
CLAMBERED	HILT	RAMSHACKLE	VENGEANCE

```
Q K M L F A C E T S L I W G Y M W C V Q U Z V M P
A Q E M F E B K M U U D L N Z A R R L K B H Q A N
X V F J J Y I O D T R W M H P J D R R U D D E R Y
O S R G R J T J M L U A I A N G U I S H R K A D K
S V Q F R F T F E I V N M O R Q R T E C C Q R D D
I L E Z C A F W A H N E I S C X V E V Z G P H N O
N B P R S L N O H L D A N C H A P O T H E C A R Y
F A E C S P A D R L T M T G Y A G X L E A N T O D
I N N T P H Y M E A K E M I E J C C O N S O L E D
R I D P X A A G B U G J R I O A M K C H A R R E D
M S U F T K T D L E R I L E U N N T L H I L T C M
A H L P H Z T N O A R K N A D O Y C G E Z X D Z K
R E U X P U Z W A W S E N G I V U B E X J S K Z S
Y D M M B Z J T K K E S D A I J O F J J N I K S G
S T A L A C T I T E S D E S A A K O M I N O U S W
```

DAY ONE

MEMORY VERSE, VOCABULARY & READING

In your reading journal, copy this week's memory verse and vocabulary definitions. Then, read chapters twenty-one and twenty-two in the book.

STORY PASSAGE

Ethan's heart leapt, and tears burst from his eyes at the familiar voice. "Sissy, I need you! Help me!"

Through his tear-filled eyes, he made out Lauren rushing forward with his shield on her arm as the bear dropped to all fours and revealed the largest woman he had ever seen behind it, holding Lauren's spear.

"No! bear eat ba'bee hoo'man!" Chief yelled as he rushed between Ethan and the bear to block the rescuers' advance. "We eat bear. Get strong."

The Bjorn-born that had faded into the trees re-appeared spears in hand.

"That is not our way," Lok called out

The Bjorn-born encircling them seemed to falter.

"Get them!" Chief threw his spear at the bear.

Lauren blocked the shot with the shield, as the giant returned fire with the spear. It caught Chief in the forehead and catapulted him to the ground behind Ethan. *That giant is powerful!*

LAUREN AND ETHAN WERE SO HAPPY TO SEE EACH OTHER! SAY A PRAYER FOR SOMEONE THAT YOU WISH YOU COULD SEE TODAY.

PASSAGE QUESTIONS

Read the STORY PASSAGE and answer the following questions in your reading journal.

1. Why did Chief want the bear to eat Ethan?
2. What words described how Ethan felt when he realized that Lauren was there?
3. Did the Bjorn-born help Chief?
4. Why did Ethan think Tye was so powerful?

Joke of the Day

My microwave started having an argument with the stove.
It got pretty heated!

DAY TWO

MEMORY VERSE, VOCABULARY & READING

In your reading journal, copy this week's memory verse and list three synonyms for each vocabulary word. Then, read chapters twenty-three and twenty-four in the book.

STORY PASSAGE

The lock and the iron around the door looked very corroded. Aiden sliced it, but this time Mother was unable to open the door. The hinges were rusted shut.

"Could we get some help?" Mother called.

"I can get it." Aiden grunted through gritted teeth as he hobbled to the other side of the door.

"Aiden, wait!" Mother rushed to his side.

He whacked the hinges, and the door slammed down, cutting off the light at the bottom. It began to tip inward toward them.

Mother tackled Aiden with a shoulder charge, his sword flung away, and it's light extinguished as it flew. They landed on the dusty floor as the door slammed behind them.

Daddy Duck flew into the warehouse and landed next to Aiden, poking Aiden's head with his bill.

"I'm OK, Daddy Duck," Aiden whispered.

First Sister spoke up, "Sisters make haste. The enemy must be alerted to our escape route."

HAVE YOU EVER BEEN TOO IMPATIENT TO STOP AND LISTEN?

PASSAGE QUESTIONS

Read the STORY PASSAGE and answer the following questions in your reading journal.

1. Why do you think Mother told Aiden to wait?
2. Why do you think Aiden didn't listen?
3. Name three things that happened because Aiden did not listen.

Joke of the Day

I picked some apples the other day
that I think are time travelers.
They're full of wormholes!

DAY THREE

MEMORY VERSE, VOCABULARY & READING

In your reading journal, copy this week's memory verse and list three antonyms for each vocabulary word. Then, read chapter twenty-five in the book.

STORY PASSAGE

Skull Crusher put the net with Ethan down—more gently than before—and opened the net all the way. Ethan had the water jug wrapped to his chest. Tye where are you?

"Get in the net!" Skull Crusher barked. Seeing how Ethan was sitting gave Lauren an idea, so she turned her belt, so the pouch with the vegetables and hidden dagger was to her front.

"What's in the bag?" Skull Crusher demanded.

Lauren reached in and pulled out a piece of carrot. "Food. Do you want to wait until we've had a full lunch, or do you want to get going?" Deep down she hoped he'd take the full lunch option.

"Sit down, before I knock you down." He demanded.

A sideways smile cracked her lips, knowing her taunting worked. He let her keep the pouch with the dagger in it. If Tye didn't come soon, she had a backup plan.

Then she sat down on the net beside Ethan with her arms wrapped around her knees. She bent over and took a sip of water from the jug Ethan was holding.

Without a word, Skull Crusher pulled the net tight and slung them over his back.

HAVE YOU EVER HAD TO DEAL WITH A BULLY?

PASSAGE QUESTIONS

Read the STORY PASSAGE and answer the following questions in your reading journal.

1. How did Lauren distract Skull Crusher from looking in her pouch?
2. Why didn't Lauren want Skull Crusher looking in her pouch?
3. Why did Lauren hope that Skull Crusher would take "the full lunch option?"
4. What do you think Lauren's backup plan was?

Joke of the Day

Did you hear that feline specialists won't shop on amazon.com? They prefer a CAT-alog!

DAY FOUR

MEMORY VERSE, VOCABULARY & READING

In your reading journal, copy this week's memory verse and draw a picture definition for each vocabulary word. Then, read chapter twenty-six in the book.

STORY PASSAGE

Mother stood. "Now we need to get out of here. What about the horses?"

Knight Protector shook his head. "There's no time to saddle them. We're just as likely to have a fall as get away cleanly."

Uncle nodded. "What're you thinkin', you old fool."

"Heath Warden, can you hide this family in the forest while I draw the enemy away?" Knight Protector started putting bit and bridle on the horses in their stalls.

"Yes! We can escape to a safe place." The giantess put her sling over her shoulder.

"I just pulled yer ragged hide out of the river. Don't go off and get yerself killed," Uncle said as he patted the old man on the shoulder.

"Go with your family and get them to Blooming Glen. All depends on it." Knight Protector shook his hand.

The kids rushed up and gave him a hug.

"Thanks for getting us this far. Mama and Uncle will get us the rest of the way." Lauren offered.

"Yes, they will, and God willing, I'll meet you there."

TELL ABOUT A TIME THAT YOU MADE A SACRIFICE FOR A FRIEND.

PASSAGE QUESTIONS

Read the STORY PASSAGE and answer the following questions in your reading journal.

1. Who are they trying to get away from?
2. What has just taken place?
3. What is Knight Protector going to do with all of the horses?
4. Why does everything depend on the family getting to Blooming Glen?

Joke of the Day

What book did Lauren get from the library for Meow Meow?
The Prince and the PAW-PURR!

DAY FIVE

READING & MEMORY VERSE

Read the epilogue in the book. Then, recite this week's memory verse aloud and complete the activity below. Include the coloring page and vocabulary puzzle with today's activities.

ACTIVITY: SALAMANDER SLIME

MATERIALS

- Elmer's white school glue, 8 oz.
- Contact saline solution, 1 1/2 Tbsp. (or more as needed)
- Baking soda, 1 Tbsp.
- Food coloring (optional)

INSTRUCTIONS

Squeeze the bottle of glue into a bowl. Add food coloring, if desired. Mix in baking soda and blend together well. (Make sure to add the food coloring before adding the contact solution!) Next, stir in the contact solution and knead until it holds together well.

If the mixture is too sticky, add more contac solution — ½ Tbsp. at a time. The contact solution changes the consistency of the mixture: more makes it thicker and less keeps it slimier.

A mat or plastic tablecloth is recommended for playing with the slime. Be careful to keep it away from hair! Recipe makes about one cup of slime.

ARMOR OF GOD

WEEK ONE
FACING TRIALS

Memory Verse:
"Finally, my brethren, be strong in the Lord, and in the power of his might. Put on the whole armor of God, that ye may be able to stand against the wiles of the devil. For we wrestle not against flesh and blood, but against principalities, against powers, against the rulers of the darkness of this world, against spiritual wickedness in high places."
— Ephesians 6:10-12 KJV

AIDEN

VOCABULARY

WORD LIST

As part of your daily work this week, you'll need to use a dictionary and a thesaurus to look up definitions, synonyms, and antonyms for the words below.

BOON COMPANION   OXIDIZED   TEMPERING

DIN   POMMEL   VISAGE

SECRET MESSAGE

This week's vocabulary words have been used to form the message below, but it's been encrypted to keep it a secret. Determine which letter in the alphabet corresponds to each number to decode the message.

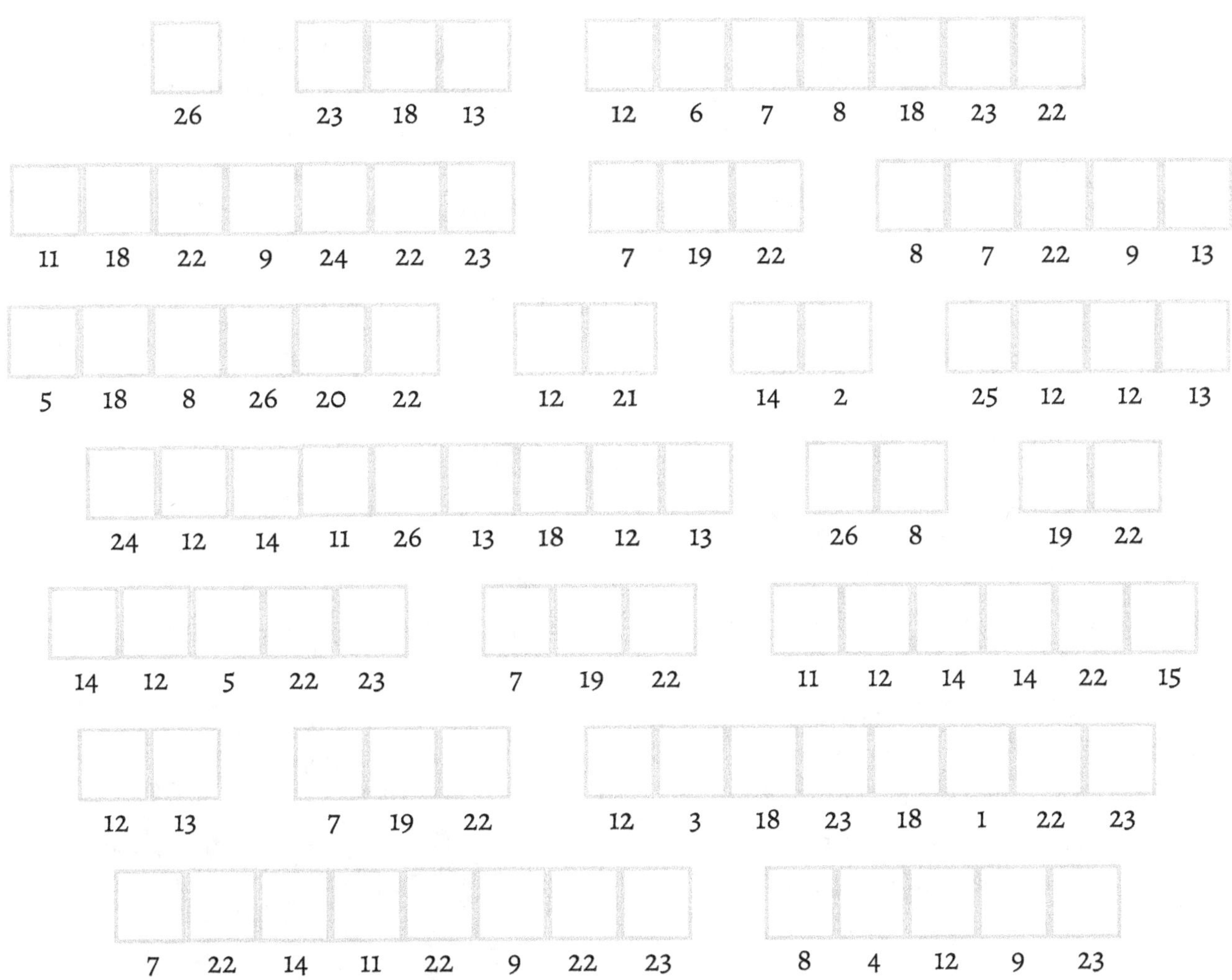

DAY ONE

MEMORY VERSE, VOCABULARY & READING

In your reading journal, copy this week's memory verse and vocabulary definitions. Then, read the prologue and chapter two in the book.

STORY PASSAGE

Mother relaxed and stared at the sky for a moment. "Take unto you the whole armor of God, that ye may be able to withstand in the evil day, and having done all, to stand. Stand therefore, having your loins girt about with truth, and having on the breastplate of righteousness; And your feet shod with the preparation of the gospel of peace; above all, taking the shield of faith, wherewith ye shall be able to quench all the fiery darts of the wicked. And take the helmet of salvation, and the sword of the Spirit, which is the word of God."

Ethan piped up, "I could sure use a helmet. I keep getting conked in the wonkus."

"Me too." Aiden nodded vigorously, and Lauren found herself doing the same.

Sparkle Frog croaked, and it made her laugh because she thought he was probably tired of healing all their bumps.

Mother's stern visage cracked, and she tousled Ethan's unruly red hair. "Yes, I guess some protection from getting conked in the wonkus might do us all some good."

She faced Uncle, "I'm sorry I was short with you. I miss him so much. I just want him back safe."

WHY IS THE ARMOR OF GOD SO IMPORTANT?

PASSAGE QUESTIONS

Read the STORY PASSAGE and answer the following questions in your reading journal.

1. Do you think the Bible verse is talking about an actual helmet that you wear?
2. In the story passage, what does "Mother's stern visage cracked" mean?
3. Why had Mother been so upset?

Joke of the Day

What's the best way to enjoy a hot dog?

By relishing it!

DAY TWO

MEMORY VERSE, VOCABULARY & READING

In your reading journal, copy this week's memory verse and list three synonyms for each vocabulary word. Then, read chapters three and four in the book.

STORY PASSAGE

"You!" Tye yelled so loud it seemed like she was right next to them. "What is this traitor doing here? He has joined forces with the dark ones!"

Skull Crusher shook his head. "Oh, you see, here she goes with the lies." He clicked his tongue as six more male giants—nearly the size of Skull Crusher—came out of the longhouse. Their stern expressions said they must be on his side.

"First, she neglects her responsibilities, allowing the child's loss. Her own brother!" He shook his head, and the giants around him joined him in their disapproval. "Then, after I save this poor wretch from a possessed bear at much personal risk, she offers to help me return the child."

"Lies!" Tye yelled.

"Silence! You were once my daughter. If you wish to live again in this village, you'll show respect to this man as he speaks!" An elder giant rebuked her.

Aiden's jaw dropped. If the elder was Tye's Father, why would he be so mean? Aiden was sure that if he was lost in the woods and then came home, his father would rush out and hug him.

HAS ANYONE EVER TOLD A LIE ABOUT YOU?

PASSAGE QUESTIONS

Read the STORY PASSAGE and answer the following questions in your reading journal.

1. In the story passage, what does "He clicked his tongue" mean?
2. What made it clear that Tye's father already believed Skull Crusher's story?
3. Why did the other giants believe Skull Crusher's story? What were some clues that the children saw on the way to Tye's village?

Joke of the Day

Why did the cowboy adopt a dachshund?
He wanted to get a long little doggy!

DAY THREE

MEMORY VERSE, VOCABULARY & READING

In your reading journal, copy this week's memory verse and list three antonyms for each vocabulary word. Then, read chapters five and six in the book.

STORY PASSAGE

"It's them!" The din of the stampeding moose drowned out the rest of Skull Crusher's call.

Aiden quickly skirted the ravine side of the fence back toward the rest of the family. Without the moose blocking the view to the clearing, he worried his flaming sword would give him away. The flames died, and he did his best to keep low as he darted back into the woods.

The crowd seemed fixated on the escaping moose. All of the men in the group, including Skull Crusher, were running at full tilt in that direction. Aiden felt the pounding of the giants' feet on the ground as they rushed away. The only people left in the clearing were Tye and her mother.

Aiden paused. Tye knelt with her hands clasped in front of her. "Mother, what he said was lies. He is of the Darkness."

Her mother knelt and hugged Tye. "I know my child, your father doesn't see it, but I do. But your case is harmed by the humans lurking in the woods." The last bit was said with emphasis. "Come out, humans. Take your companion and be off."

WHY IMPORTANT IS IT TO BE ABLE TO TRUST YOUR PARENTS?

PASSAGE QUESTIONS

Read the STORY PASSAGE and answer the following questions in your reading journal.

1. In the story passage, what does "running at full tilt in that direction" mean?
2. Why does Tye's mother say "your is case harmed by the humans lurking in the woods"?
3. Who is the "companion" Tye's mother is referring to?

Joke of the Day

What did the French fry say to its friend?

Let's ketchup later.

DAY FOUR

MEMORY VERSE, VOCABULARY & READING

In your reading journal, copy this week's memory verse and draw a picture definition for each vocabulary word. Then, read chapters seven and eight in the book.

STORY PASSAGE

"Scarface, get that axe! It's got to be one of the special weapons we're supposed to return to the mountain." One of the Steele Brothers called from behind.

"Yes, First Brother." Another voice responded.

Uncle froze. That axe meant the difference between life and death in the wilderness. Without it, he couldn't build shelter, make fire, or defend himself. Plus, it was... special... his brother had given it to him. He couldn't let it fall into the enemy's hands.

Uncle turned to see three Steele Brothers, sledgehammers in hand, continuing to carefully pick their way down the hill, and the third rummaged in the brush off the path.

"I got it!" he called as he lifted Ol'Faithful from the ground. "Arrgh! it burns!" He immediately dropped it.

From a distance, Uncle couldn't tell what happened, but as the rain came down in the Steele Brother's open hands, it appeared that rust-colored liquid began rolling off Scarface's palms.

The other Steele Brothers stopped cold to look at their companion. The Light wasn't going to let the minions of Darkness just take his axe. If they got burned picking it up, then the rest of the weapons would likely have the same effect.

HAVE YOU EVER LOST SOMETHING THAT WAS SPECIAL TO YOU?

PASSAGE QUESTIONS

Read the STORY PASSAGE and answer the following questions in your reading journal.

1. How do you think Uncle felt when he lost Ol'Faithful?
2. Why is Ol'Faithful so important to Uncle?
3. What happened when Scarface picked up Ol'Faithful? Why do you think it happened?

Joke of the Day

What does a cat say after a joke?
Just kitten!

DAY FIVE

READING & MEMORY VERSE

Read chapters nine and ten in the book. Then, recite this week's memory verse aloud and complete the activity below. Include the coloring page and vocabulary puzzle with today's activities.

ACTIVITY: SHIELD OF FAITH

MATERIALS

- Large piece of cardboard
- Duct tape
- Strong scissors (or box cutter with adult supervision)
- Pencil & tape measure
- Tempera paints

INSTRUCTIONS

1. Decide the width of your shield by holding up the cardboard against your body. Measure how long across you want the top to be, and make a mark on each side of the cardboard. Draw a vertical line from each mark down to the bottom of the cardboard.
2. Decide the length of your shield, and draw a horizontal line across the bottom of your cardboard. You should now have a rectangle.
3. To make a shield shape, measure the bottom line to find the center and mark it. Draw arched lines from the center mark to the top corners of the rectangle.
4. Cut out a thick rectangular strip of cardboard for the handle and duct tape the edges to the back of your shield.
5. Paint your shield however you wish!

A shield can be maneuvered to cover chinks in a warrior's armor and deflect arrows. Great warriors are skilled at using their shields to keep themselves safe from harm. The Shield of Faith requires the same treatment.

HOW DO YOU USE YOUR FAITH TO PROTECT YOURSELF IN THE WORLD?

WEEK TWO
SEEKING TRUTH

Memory Verse:

"Wherefore take unto you the whole armor of God, that ye may be able to withstand in the evil day, and having done all, to stand. Stand therefore, having your loins girt about with truth, and having on the breastplate of righteousness;"
—Ephesians 6:13-14

ETHAN

VOCABULARY

WORD LIST

As part of your daily work this week, you'll need to use a dictionary and a thesaurus to look up definitions, synonyms, and antonyms for the words below.

ARSENAL

BLIGHTER

GRIMACED

NOXIOUS

QUARTERSTAFF

RAUCOUS

WORD SCRAMBLE

Rearrange each group of letters below to unscramble the words.

SOUCARU

__ __ __ __ __ __ __

TRFUASQREAFT

__ __ __ __ __ __ __ __ __ __ __ __

RACMIEGD

__ __ __ __ __ __ __ __

NSLAAER

__ __ __ __ __ __ __

TRHIGEBL

__ __ __ __ __ __ __ __

SIOONXU

__ __ __ __ __ __ __

DAY ONE

MEMORY VERSE, VOCABULARY & READING

In your reading journal, copy this week's memory verse and vocabulary definitions. Then, read chapter eleven and twelve in the book.

STORY PASSAGE

She patted him on the head. "Dear boy, if you are anything like your brother, you think opposing us is the righteous thing to do." She gestured toward First Brother, who stood on the platform and held Ethan's shield with the shovel. "So we'll disabuse you of that notion and then let you free." She walked up the ramp to the censer, and two metal men carrying hay bale hooks in each hand followed her.

A chill flowed down Ethan's spine. He didn't know what she was talking about, but it didn't sound good. He was stuck. There was no good way out of the rope tying his hands. Chief was still free, but there were too many warriors for just the two of them without his shield. How could he shine his light like this?

Feeling defeated, he slumped, accepting the thorns poking into his back. His arms slid down the pole, his ropes snagging a thorn. He wriggled around a bit and found a spot to get most of the thorns out of his back while slowly running the cord tying his hands over the thorn. I might be able to get out!

HOW DO YOU FIND HOPE IN WHAT SEEMS LIKE HOPELESS SITUATIONS?

PASSAGE QUESTIONS

Read the STORY PASSAGE and answer the following questions in your reading journal.

1. What did Prime Sister mean when she said, "So we'll disabuse you of that notion and then let you free"?
2. What is Ethan's plan to get free?
3. What do you think they are going to do with Ethan's shield?

Joke of the Day

Why do elephants love swimming pools?
They always have their trunks with them!

DAY TWO

MEMORY VERSE, VOCABULARY & READING

In your reading journal, copy this week's memory verse and list three synonyms for each vocabulary word. Then, read chapters thirteen and fourteen in the book.

STORY PASSAGE

Hot tears burst from Ethan's eyes as he saw his shield now had uneven chunks of metal covering the bottom half of it, and the shine was gone from the top half. "You ruined it!" She shook her head, "Oh no, little one, it is now a perfect weapon of the true light." At that, pieces of the jagged metal took on a hint of a red glow. She put her arm through the straps and showed it to First Brother. "Now, who's the ignorant girl?"

"You are!" Mother's voice rang out from across the courtyard. "That's no weapon of the True Light! This is!" Ethan turned his head toward the gate and caught the green light of Mother's blade from the corner of his eye.

Ethan snapped his head back to look at Prime Sister, "You're in big trouble now! My Mama's gonna get you!" Ethan kept up trying to cut his rope. The thorns were almost through.

Prime Sister's mouth dropped open for a moment, then she recovered, "Brothers, to arms! We need the girl and her mother alive!" She leapt from the platform.

PASSAGE QUESTIONS

Read the STORY PASSAGE and answer the following questions in your reading journal.

1. How does Ethan feel when he sees his shield?
2. How do his emotions change when Mother shows up?
3. Predict what will happen in this confrontation. If you have already read the whole chapter, were you surprised at what happened?

Joke of the Day

Why was Cinderella so hopeful about her photos?
She knew her prints would come.

DAY THREE

MEMORY VERSE, VOCABULARY & READING

In your reading journal, copy this week's memory verse and list three antonyms for each vocabulary word. Then, read chapters fifteen and sixteen in the book.

STORY PASSAGE

"Aiden! Sword!" Chief called back, still holding the flint knife.

Terror gripped Aiden's chest. If Chief cut the cord, he'd be lost with the Bjorn-born. *God, please help me.*

He reached under the water and pulled his sword free. It came out of the river in a poof of fire and steam. The puff of hot vapor surprised him, and he lost grip on the log. The river's current slammed him into the cord, knocking the air out of him as he sank.

He reached for the cord with his free hand and missed. In his desperation to grab the rope, he dropped his sword. It sank like a rock, lost in the depths, as Aiden struggled to stay afloat. Out of the corner of his eye, he saw Chief with his arm raised, ready to strike the cord with his knife. *No! I've failed Chief's people.*

HOW DO YOU ASK FOR GOD'S HELP WHEN YOU FEEL LIKE YOU HAVE DISAPPOINTED SOMEONE?

PASSAGE QUESTIONS

Read the STORY PASSAGE and answer the following questions in your reading journal.

1. Why is Chief preparing to cut the cord with his knife?
2. What happens to Aiden's sword?
3. How did you feel at the end of this chapter?

Joke of the Day

What do you call a food truck that only serves dessert?
A sweet ride!

DAY FOUR

MEMORY VERSE, VOCABULARY & READING

In your reading journal, copy this week's memory verse and draw a picture definition for each vocabulary word. Then, read chapters seventeen and eighteen in the book.

STORY PASSAGE

She bowed her head. "No, my lord, I can handle caring for the boy. But his shoes are destroyed, and one foot is badly burned. We need clean dressings and ointment to keep him from getting infected when we travel."

"It's going to be a long trek to Spring Fields; we don't have time to waste on such niceties." Refi'Cul leaned the spear against the crate and then picked up the crowbar from where he'd dropped it earlier. He fished into the box with it and pulled out a little pair of very plain-looking, brown leather boots tied together by the laces. He flicked the boots to Prime Sister. "These will have to do."

Ethan's eyes got big. Did Daddy make him boots too? What do they do?

Nursemaid turned them over in her hands, "My lord, are you sure that's a good idea? These boots were in with powerful weapons and armor. Are you sure they don't have a power of their own?"

"All of these weapons are of the finest craftsmanship; the boots look like they came from the village cobbler." He scoffed. "Nothing more than a father's gift to his son, wouldn't you say?"

DO YOU THINK THAT PEOPLE CAN LEARN FROM THEIR MISTAKES?

PASSAGE QUESTIONS

Read the STORY PASSAGE and answer the following questions in your reading journal.

1. Do you think Prime Sister will be a good nursemaid to Ethan?
2. What do you think about the pair of boots that Refi'Cul took out of the crate?
3. Is Refi'Cul making a mistake by giving the boots to Ethan?

DAY FIVE

READING & MEMORY VERSE

Read chapters nineteen and twenty in the book. Then, recite this week's memory verse aloud and complete the activity below. Include the coloring page and vocabulary puzzle with today's activities.

ACTIVITY: SWORD OF THE SPIRIT

MATERIALS

- Cardboard
- Pencil & ruler
- Strong scissors (or box cutter to be used with adult supervision)
- Tin foil

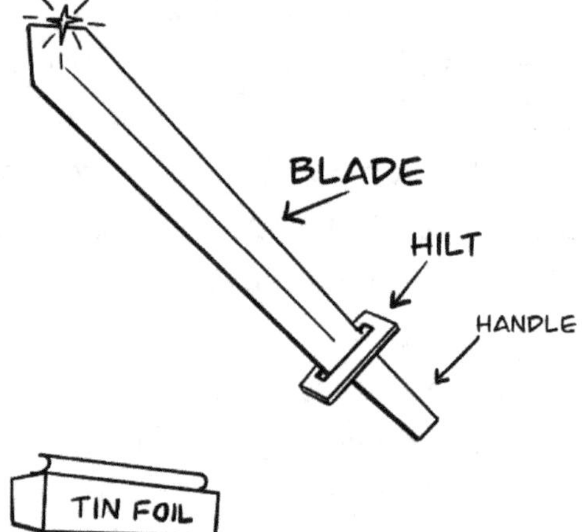

INSTRUCTIONS

1. Use the pencil and the ruler to draw the shape of your sword and handle.
2. Next, use them to draw a hilt. (Note: This is just a large rectangle with a small rectangle drawn inside it.) Cut out around the outside and the inside lines. You will be left with a rectangle-shaped hole in the middle that should be just large enough to fit over your sword handle.
3. Cut out your sword and hilt. Place the hilt over the sword handle.
4. Cover the sword blade in tin foil to make it shiny.

HOW DO YOU USE THE SWORD OF THE SPIRIT, WHICH IS THE WORD OF GOD, IN YOUR DAILY LIFE?

WEEK THREE
SHARING FAITH

Memory Verse:

"The night is far spent, the day is at hand: let us therefore cast off the works of darkness, and let us put on the armor of light."
—Romans 13:12

LAUREN

VOCABULARY

WORD LIST

As part of your daily work this week, you'll need to use a dictionary and a thesaurus to look up definitions, synonyms, and antonyms for the words below.

CONCUSSIVE	GARRISON	REVERIE
FRACAS	GEYSER	WINCED

MAZE

Help the kids find their way! Trace a path from the center of the maze to the outside.

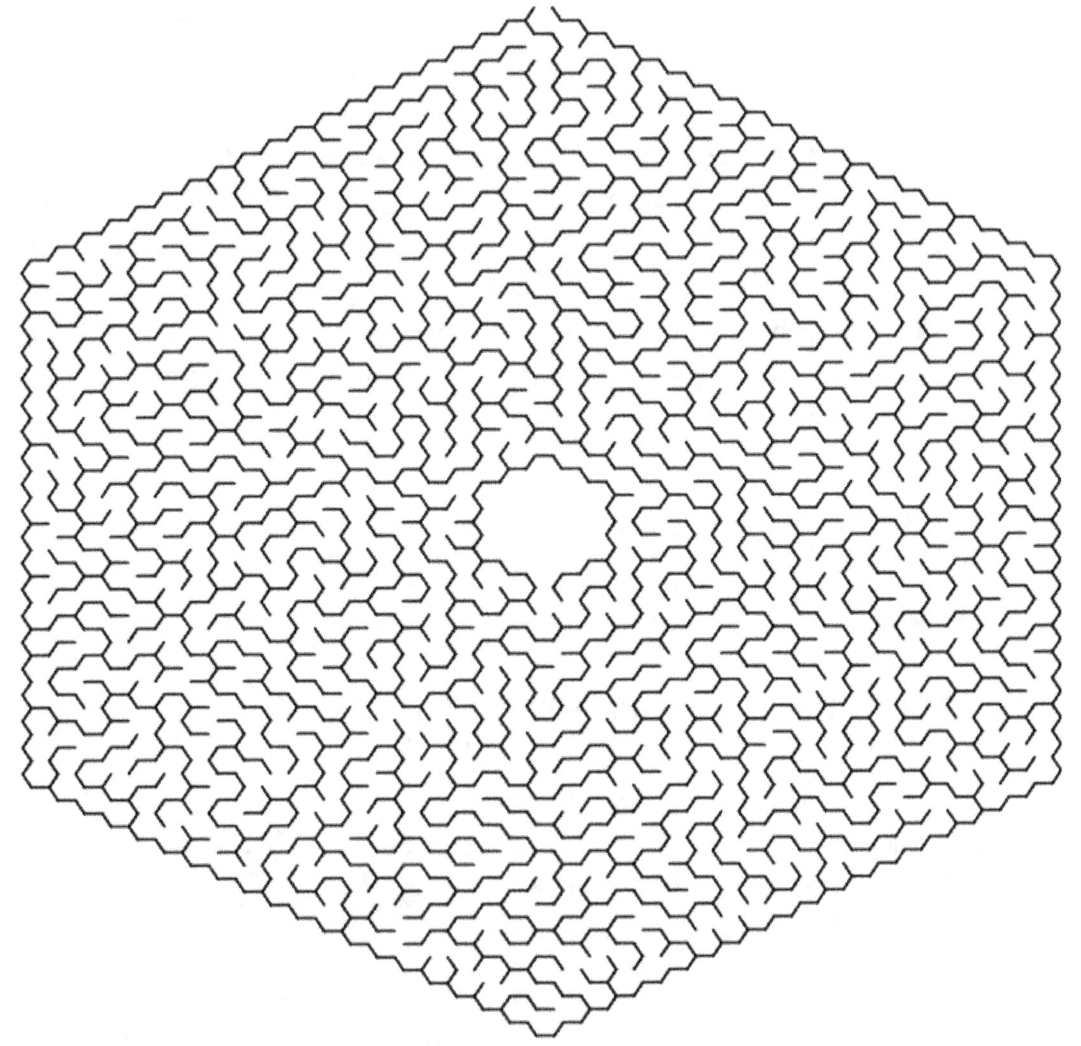

DAY ONE

MEMORY VERSE, VOCABULARY & READING

In your reading journal, copy this week's memory verse and vocabulary definitions. Then, read chapters twenty-one and twenty-two in the book.

STORY PASSAGE

"What's that?" Aiden moved to look at the paper.

Uncle unfolded it to reveal a sheet of paper the size of a wall map. He had to hold it out in front of him at arm's length to look at the whole thing. In the upper corner, it said "Armor of God." Then, there were images of various weapons and pieces of armor broken apart and marked with measurements.

"Well, I'll be. Its plans. Plans fer all the different weapons yer father made. With this and the right kind of forge, we could make me a new axe and you a new sword. Look over there in the lower left that looks like yer sword."

Aiden's eyes went wide at the sight of his sword broken down into the pieces used to make it. He scanned the page, found Lauren's spear, Uncle's axe, Mother's dagger, and Ethan's shield. There were other things like the belt and some boots, a breastplate, some different helmets—even a little drawing of some horseshoes.

Aiden remembered Father reading them the verse from the Good Book about the whole armor of God. Looking at the plans, it seemed like Father had designed a complete set for the entire family. But where was it?

TALK ABOUT SOMETHING THAT MAKES YOU FEEL HOPEFUL.

PASSAGE QUESTIONS

Read the STORY PASSAGE and answer the following questions in your reading journal.

1. How did Aiden and Uncle feel when they found Father's plans?
2. Where did Father get the idea for his plans?
3. Do you think they will be able to make more armor now that they have the plans?

Joke of the Day

I got lost in the rainforest and I needed supplies.
So, I ordered from Amazon!

DAY TWO

MEMORY VERSE, VOCABULARY & READING

In your reading journal, copy this week's memory verse and list three synonyms for each vocabulary word. Then, read chapters twenty-three and twenty-four in the book.

STORY PASSAGE

Nothing happened. They sat there for a full minute just waiting and watching, and the bump was still there. A chill raced down Lauren's spine. She wasn't sure if it was from the dark, damp air of the cave or dread that Tye wasn't waking.

Lauren knelt next to Sparkle Frog. "Hey, little buddy, what's going on? Is it something about this cave?"

Sparkle Frog croaked and then leapt across the cave and onto the ledge. His signature rainbow arc trailed through the air behind him.

Aiden's head shaking was barely visible in the low light of the cave. "I don't think that's it. He can light up even in this dark place. Plus, with the censer gone, this is the most light we've had in a long time."

"I wonder if it's the spear," Lauren said haltingly.

Aiden cocked his head. "What do you mean?"

"Well, they corrupted my spear, and Refi'Cul knocked out Tye with it. Maybe it's some kind of Darkness wound." Lauren bent down to inspect it, but she couldn't see very well in the dim light.

WHAT DO YOU DO WHEN THINGS DON'T SEEM RIGHT?

PASSAGE QUESTIONS

Read the STORY PASSAGE and answer the following questions in your reading journal.

1. What happened when Aiden put Sparkle Frog on Tye's head?
2. Do you think the reason Sparkle Frog can't help Tye's bump is because of the cave?
3. Do you think Tye will be the same when she wakes up?

Joke of the Day

How does a cabin get on the internet?
It logs in!

DAY THREE

MEMORY VERSE, VOCABULARY & READING

In your reading journal, copy this week's memory verse and list three antonyms for each vocabulary word. Then, read chapters twenty-five and twenty-six in the book.

STORY PASSAGE

Mother stepped up next to Lauren. "Tok, I don't know if I can explain this in a way you'll understand." She put her hand on Tok's heart. "I know you're angry with your father about the Darkness. You feel like he let it in your village."

"Yes, Fader bring Darkness." Tok nodded with squinted eyes.

"But he changed. They helped him change." She pointed to Lauren and Tye. "He was ready to fight to take your village back."

"Yeah, we were going to get the metal men. Weren't we, Uncle?" Aiden added, and Uncle nodded.

"So, are you disobeying because you are angry?" Mother waited a long time, staring into Tok's eyes.

"No, Tok sad." A tear formed on his cheek. "E'tan lost, Tok help."

Mother took the robe she'd thrown over her shoulder and wiped his tear away. "OK. Is disobeying your father the best way to help Ethan?"

HAVE YOU EVER DISOBEYED YOUR PARENTS BECAUSE YOU THOUGHT YOU WERE TRYING TO HELP A FRIEND?

PASSAGE QUESTIONS

Read the STORY PASSAGE and answer the following questions in your reading journal.

1. Why was Tok so angry?
2. Why did Tok really want to go with them into the Darkness?
3. How does Mother help Ethan understand that he needs to obey his father?

Joke of the Day

What makes a game of bingo lifeless?
Lack of O2.

DAY FOUR

MEMORY VERSE, VOCABULARY & READING

In your reading journal, copy this week's memory verse and draw a picture definition for each vocabulary word. Then, read chapters twenty-seven and twenty-eight in the book.

STORY PASSAGE

Ethan's mouth dropped open, and a chill wracked his body. If he shined his light, Daddy might go poof into dust, just like the Steele Brothers did.

Champion pointed his wounded hand at the soldiers in the stable. "If I gently tap one of those fools with this sword while they're wearing that armor, they'll turn to rust. That's what it has to 'do with this.'"

He faced Refi'Cul. "So where's the censer? The only way I can fix this is to melt it all back down and re-work it."

Refi'Cul took a step back and looked at his feet.

A huge smile broke out on Ethan's face as he said, "Refi'Cul broke it with Sissy's spear."

"What?" Champion whirled to Ethan.

"Yeah, he thought he was going to be all scary and stuff and break the lantern, but then broke the platform the censer was on, and it just poured out everywhere." Ethan wished he could see the actual look on Father's face rather than just his eyes through the mask. He was pretty sure if Father's metal face could get red, it would be right now.

WHEN IS TELLING THE TRUTH EASY AND WHEN IS IT DIFFICULT?

PASSAGE QUESTIONS

Read the STORY PASSAGE and answer the following questions in your reading journal.

1. How is Refi'Cul's idea to have Ethan tell Champion what happened backfiring?
2. What does Ethan learn about the armor that the Steele Brothers corrupted?
3. How do you know Ethan enjoys telling Father the story?

DAY FIVE

READING & MEMORY VERSE

Read chapters twenty-nine and thirty in the book. Then, recite this week's memory verse aloud and complete the activity below. Include the coloring page and vocabulary puzzle with today's activities.

ACTIVITY: LAUREN'S SPEAR

MATERIALS

- Old broomstick or mopstick
- Pencil & ruler
- Pool noodle
- Duct tape
- Serrated knife (or box cutter with adult supervision)

INSTRUCTIONS

1. Unscrew the broom or mop from the stick.
2. Cut off about a foot of your pool noodle.
3. Use your ruler and pencil to draw a pointed spear shape at the end of the pool noodle.
4. Cut out the spear shape, cutting all the way through the noodle. Be sure to leave 4-5 inches at the bottom of the noodle intact.
5. Place your spear shape onto the stick, point up, and tape it on with duct tape. Start by winding the duct tape around the stick below the noodle, then wind it up and around the base of the noodle several times. Go up a few inches on the base of the noodle to secure it firmly.
6. Duct tape the point together by placing a piece of duct tape down on each slanted side of the point of the spear.
7. If you want to cover your entire spear with duct tape that's fine as well. Choose whatever color of duct tape you'd like your spear to be.

LAUREN ALWAYS USES HER SPEAR TO PROTECT HER FRIENDS AND FAMILY. HOW DOES GOD HELP YOU PROTECT THE PEOPLE YOU CARE ABOUT?

WEEK FOUR
PERSEVERING

Memory Verse:
*"Be of good courage, and he shall strengthen your heart,
all ye that hope in the Lord."*
— Psalms 31:24

ETHAN

VOCABULARY

WORD LIST

As part of your daily work this week, you'll need to use a dictionary and a thesaurus to look up definitions, synonyms, and antonyms for the words below.

ABSOLVE   PALL   SHACKLES
CACHE   PASSEL   SHODDY

WORD SEARCH

Find and circle the hidden vocabulary words in the puzzle below. Words may appear up, down, forwards, backwards, or diagonally.

ABSOLVE	DIN	OXIDIZED	REVERIE
ARSENAL	FRACAS	PALL	SHACKLES
BLIGHTER	GARRISON	PASSEL	SHODDY
BOON COMPANION	GEYSER	POMMEL	TEMPERING
CACHE	GRIMACED	QUARTERSTAFF	VISAGE
CONCUSSIVE	NOXIOUS	RAUCOUS	WINCED

```
R C O N C U S S I V E W I N C E D E U P Z P T L A
S C P Y I H L C O C Y F R A C A S Z P O G D I N R
T K O N K Q S A T K T D L S K D Y Q H M N K P N S
L E G Y W I P C B L I G H T E R K J C M O J W R E
F K U W P B X H G Q V I A N D U J U K E O J M E N
G E Y S E R V E R F U B Q Y U G H F N L F E N V A
Q H W O B S G H I B O O N C O M P A N I O N O E L
Z W R X J H A P M D E D S Y K V I S A G E U X R D
T G A I E A R R A Q U A R T E R S T A F F C I I E
P G U D I C R I C A W P X A J U B G A X I V O E S
A Y C I S K I Z E Q J A B S O L V E K L D X U U H
L U O Z G L S E D R E A P F D K S G L W U U S R O
L Q U E W E O T I E Y D L H P D P A S S E L L S D
L I S D E S N I R K Z J C S P R E Z H T B M Z S D
T E M P E R I N G U B Z K K P H T Q R P O S M Y Y
```

DAY ONE

MEMORY VERSE, VOCABULARY & READING

In your reading journal, copy this week's memory verse and vocabulary definitions. Then, read chapters thirty-one and thirty-two in the book.

STORY PASSAGE

Lauren had Aiden help make room for Tye to ride with them in the wagon. Lauren hoped this would give her a chance to talk to her friend and maybe cheer her up. But Tye had refused and ran next to the horses instead. Lauren couldn't figure it out. Perhaps she was punishing herself for the actions of her people. Maybe she blamed Lauren for all her troubles. It hurt Lauren to have her friend reject all her attempts to help.

By noon on the second day, Tye started losing ground and began trailing the wagon. Mother finally ordered the giantess to ride with them. Lauren thought now she might be able to connect with Tye. But the giantess just chose to sit in sullen silence. Any attempts to talk to her were met with no response.

Lauren took the step to put Meow Meow in Tye's lap, and she did slowly pet the kitten while staring off into space. Lauren tried putting an arm around her friend in support. Tye didn't object to that, but she didn't lean into Lauren, either. It was almost like Lauren wasn't even there.

At least she was no longer rejecting Lauren outright.

HOW DO YOU PRAY FOR A FRIEND IN NEED?

PASSAGE QUESTIONS

Read the STORY PASSAGE and answer the following questions in your reading journal.

1. What happened when Lauren and Aiden made room for Tye to ride in the wagon?
2. Give some examples of how Tye is treating Lauren differently?
3. Why do you think Tye is acting this way?

Joke of the Day

What's the longest word in the dictionary?
Smiles. Because there is a mile between the s's.

DAY TWO

MEMORY VERSE, VOCABULARY & READING

In your reading journal, copy this week's memory verse and list three synonyms for each vocabulary word. Then, read chapters thirty-three and thirty-four in the book.

STORY PASSAGE

Ethan belted out, "This little light of mine!" And his eyes went wide as Lauren and Aiden stood up in the back of the wagon to join him in the song. Aiden had something in his hand that he threw at Champion.

"No!" Ethan gripped the wheelbarrow's handles and pushed it faster than he ever thought possible. It connected with the back of Champion's knees just as the purple bomb splatted on the top of his helmet.

Father fell into the wheelbarrow while Ethan's siblings sang, "I'm gonna let it shine." Light erupted all around, illuminating the intersection.

The Steele Brother driving the wagon poofed into red dust as Champion burst into flame.

"No! Daddy!" Ethan planted his feet to stop.

"Run straight to the lake!" Iron Sister called.

Ethan's feet throbbed with power like when he was holding his shield. Daddy must have made these special boots for him too! He poured on the speed and rocketed down the cobblestone street, nearly dumping the wheelbarrow over multiple times as the flames fanned back toward him.

HOW DO YOU RELY ON GOD'S STRENGTH?

PASSAGE QUESTIONS

Read the STORY PASSAGE and answer the following questions in your reading journal.

1. What surprised Ethan as he sang?
2. How did Ethan help Father?
3. Why didn't Father turn to dust like the other Steele Brothers?

Joke of the Day

What vegetable did Noah leave off the ark?

The leek.

DAY THREE

MEMORY VERSE, VOCABULARY & READING

In your reading journal, copy this week's memory verse and list three antonyms for each vocabulary word. Then, read chapters thirty-five and thirty-six in the book.

STORY PASSAGE

Uncle led Knight Protector and Iron Sister up the hill and into the night, visible only by their flaming swords.

Ethan and Aiden took turns breaking the corruption on the armor and weapons, trying to see who could get the biggest poof.

Mother stood at the back of the wagon, her tears falling on Father's face.

"Mother, is there such a thing as the Wellspring of Life?" Lauren said with her heart in her throat.

Mother snuffled up her tears, "Understanding is a wellspring of life unto him that hath it." She locked her tear-filled eyes with Lauren, "Why are you asking?"

Lauren held up the faintly glowing snow globe, "I mean, is it a real thing, like the Armor of God? If it were real, would water from the Wellspring of Life save Father?"

Mother put an arm around Lauren's shoulder and hugged her tight as tears ran down her face. "Yes, it is very real, and God willing, your father will drink the living waters before it's too late."

WHEN YOU HAVE DOUBTS, HOW DO YOU REMEMBER THAT GOD CAN DO THE IMPOSSIBLE?

PASSAGE QUESTIONS

Read the STORY PASSAGE and answer the following questions in your reading journal.

1. How are Aiden and Ethan "breaking the corruption on the armor and weapons"?
2. Why is Lauren asking Mother about the Wellspring of Life?
3. What does Mother say is going to save Father?

Joke of the Day

I know a lot about ice cream.
I spent years in sundae school.

DAY FOUR

MEMORY VERSE, VOCABULARY & READING

In your reading journal, copy this week's memory verse and draw a picture definition for each vocabulary word. Then, read the epilogue in the book.

STORY PASSAGE

Bishop scanned around the room. "Where is Champion? We need to start building censers right away."

Refi'Cul smoothed out the censer plans on the table. "He's out verifying some measurements. He didn't know how to convert these symbols to modern dimensions."

"Ahh this must be in kadans. It's a base-sixty system. Very confusing to the novice. Champion was right to try to check his conversions. But I need no verification." Bishop scooped up the plans and pulled a Y'lohnu globe from his pocket.

"I took a big risk traveling here with the Y'lohnu globe. This was our last." He held the orb up to Refi'Cul's eyes. "But now that I have the plans and the mountain, I'll never run out, and the true light will cloak the land.

"When Champion returns, set him to making weapons. Then join me at the mountain and bring the giants. In ten days, I'll have enough censers to blot out that cursed Tower of Light forever."

WHAT CAN YOU DO TO FIGHT THE DARKNESS IN OUR WORLD?

PASSAGE QUESTIONS

Read the STORY PASSAGE and answer the following questions in your reading journal.

1. How does Refi'Cul really feel about Bishop?
2. Now that Bishop has the plans to make more censers, what do you think this will mean for The Heathlands?
3. What do you think will happen when Bishop finds out that they lost their Champion?

DAY FIVE

READING & MEMORY VERSE

Congratulations on finishing the book! Today, recite this week's memory verse aloud and complete the activity below. Include the coloring page and vocabulary puzzle with today's activities.

ACTIVITY: GOD'S CHANGE

MATERIALS

- Dirty pennies
- Clear bowl
- 1 Tsp. salt
- 4 tbsp. white vinegar
- Disposable gloves
- Paper towels
- Spoon

INSTRUCTIONS

1. Mix the salt and white vinegar in the clear bowl.
2. The pennies represent people in the world. We get messy on the inside and the outside. Drop the pennies into the solution.
3. The solution represents having a relationship with God, and how we are changed by Him. Stir the pennies around for a little over a minute and remove them with gloves on. Then, dry them with a paper towel. Notice the difference!
4. God doesn't just change us on the outside, but on the inside as well. Our outward appearance and actions change for the better as God changes our hearts!

Just like Aiden and Ethan used their Holy weapons to change the corrupted armor, Jesus changes our hearts when we choose to have a relationship with Him.

HOW HAS GOD CHANGED YOU?

WELLSPRING OF LIFE

WEEK ONE
NEW STRATEGIES

Memory Verse:
"Keep thy heart with all diligence;
For out of it are the issues of life."
—Proverbs 4:23 KJV

ETHAN

VOCABULARY

WORD LIST

As part of your daily work this week, you'll need to use a dictionary and a thesaurus to look up definitions, synonyms, and antonyms for the words below.

BEFALL   EXASPERATED   PRONTO
CACOPHONY   IRONY   RESPITE

SECRET MESSAGE

This week's vocabulary words have been used to form the message below, but it's been encrypted to keep it a secret. Determine which letter in the alphabet corresponds to each number to decode the message.

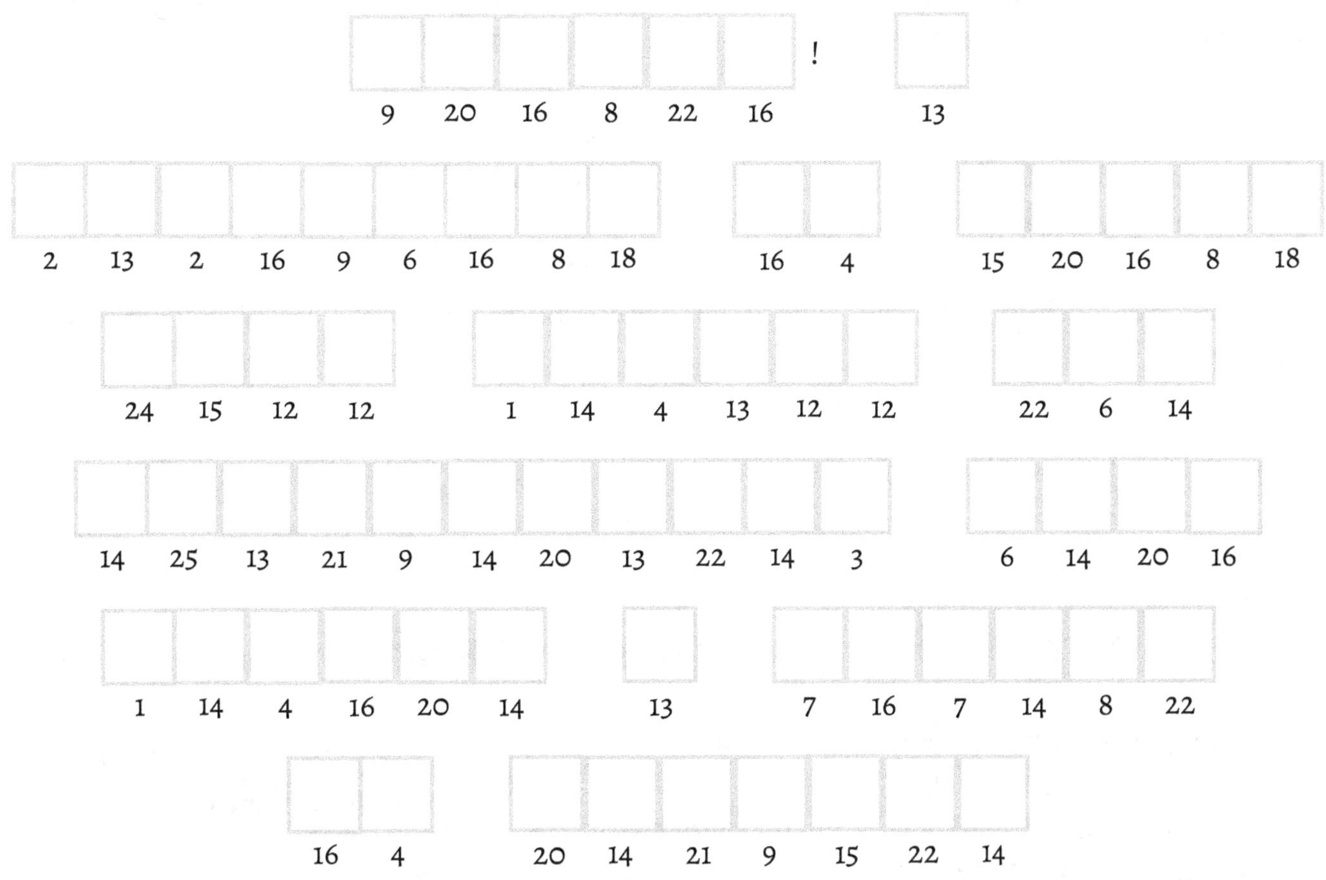

DAY ONE

MEMORY VERSE, VOCABULARY & READING

In your reading journal, copy this week's memory verse and vocabulary definitions. Then, read chapters one and two in the book.

STORY PASSAGE

"Oh no!" Ethan whispered. "They must have found my tracks somehow." He held up his palm toward her. "I can't take your lantern. I think you're going to need it to protect your family. Maybe I can find one of the other ones he gave out."

"Many families have fled the city, going north to Blooming Glen." She gestured toward her front window, then the far wall. "Others have gone West to the springs at Bubbling Wine. We stay because my parents feel our mission is here despite the Darkness."

Ethan's heart swelled in his chest. Knowing other Light Bearers were out there gave him confidence. However, he was worried about the giants turning around and needed to go. "Do you have a back door?"

"Yes, through there." She pointed down the hallway behind them.

Ethan stood up. "I'm going to go and draw them away."

The little girl's brow furrowed, and Ethan could tell she was worried.

"Thank you for shining your light." Ethan stared into her eyes. "We'll come back for you with lots of help once we help Daddy and shine the Light in Blooming Glen. I promise."

WHY IS IT GOOD TO HAVE FRIENDS TO BACK YOU UP?

PASSAGE QUESTIONS

Read the STORY PASSAGE and answer the following questions in your reading journal.

1. In the passage, what are some clues that Ethan wanted to protect Sarah?
2. How did Ethan feel when he learned there were other Light Bearers?
3. How do you know Sarah is also fighting the Darkness?

> **Joke of the Day**
>
> How do you know if a pool is safe for diving?
>
> It deep-ends!

DAY TWO

MEMORY VERSE, VOCABULARY & READING

In your reading journal, copy this week's memory verse and list three synonyms for each vocabulary word. Then, read chapter three in the book.

STORY PASSAGE

"If you want my help, I'll have no more talk of attacking my people."

Lauren was stunned by this. Tye was cast out of her village based on Skull Crusher's lies. It was so cruel, and her own father had made it clear she was unwanted. So why would Tye feel any loyalty to them? Didn't Tye see this was her family now?

"But—" Uncle's reply was cut short by Mother holding up her hand.

"Tye, you are right. I was there." Mother took a knee next to Father. "Skull Crusher deceived them, and he, in turn, has been deceived by the Bishop. Our fight is with the Bishop and Refi'Cul, not the Heath Wardens."

Iron Sister chimed in, "Which is why I must go a different path."
"What?" Ethan blurted out from the back of the wagon. "No, you need to help us. You're my Iron Sister."

Lauren knew Ethan had become fond of Iron Sister, but she didn't realize how this might just break his heart.

"I will help you, little brother," Iron Sister responded. "I need to gather the Iron Priestesses for battle against Refi'Cul and the Bishop."

WHY IS IT HARD TO FORGIVE OTHERS FOR THEIR ACTIONS?

PASSAGE QUESTIONS

Read the STORY PASSAGE and answer the following questions in your reading journal.

1. How did Mother help Lauren understand Tye's feelings after the way her family treated her?
2. How does Ethan feel about Iron Sister leaving the group? Do you think it is a good idea?

Joke of the Day

Why did the camera stop dreaming about a photography career?
He couldn't remain focused.

DAY THREE

MEMORY VERSE, VOCABULARY & READING

In your reading journal, copy this week's memory verse and list three antonyms for each vocabulary word. Then, read chapters four and five in the book.

STORY PASSAGE

"I will do this . . . without delay," Tye said with a cold snap in her voice. Aiden couldn't tell if she was mad at them for some reason, or if she was being cold because she didn't really want to leave them.

Regardless, the giantess turned to the general direction of the Censer Uncle indicated on the slate. Aiden agreed it was the right thing to do, but something felt . . . off. Was his map correct? A slight miscalculation here could put her way off course. "Wait, Tye! You'll have a better direction if you wait until we destroy the next Censer."

She paused for a moment, staring off in the distance, standing stone cold, still as a statue.

Lauren ran to her and grabbed her hand. "Maybe we can find horses or something between here and there, so you don't have to go alone."

The way Lauren was pleading with Tye, told Aiden his sister hadn't completely bought into the plan to send Tye off on her own. However, a groan from Father punctuated the urgency for action. They were going to have to find a way to destroy that other Censer, or Father wouldn't make it to the Wellspring of Life. Would they find a way to send someone with Tye or risk her going it alone?

HAVE YOU EVER HAD TO REBUILD YOUR TRUST IN SOMEONE?

PASSAGE QUESTIONS

Read the STORY PASSAGE and answer the following questions in your reading journal.

1. What are some clues that Aiden and Lauren don't want Tye going off on her own?
2. In the passage, what does "punctuated the urgency for action" mean?
3. Why do they feel Tye going off alone is a risk?

Joke of the Day

How do bears communicate?

Teddy-grahams!

DAY FOUR

MEMORY VERSE, VOCABULARY & READING

In your reading journal, copy this week's memory verse and draw a picture definition for each vocabulary word. Then, read chapters six and seven in the book.

STORY PASSAGE

"That general direction huh." Gramps got to his feet and tried to dust off his hands on his pants, but just kicked up more dust and coughed before continuing, "Well there's this grove of the high and mighty or some such in that general direction."

Mother raised an eyebrow and looked at Uncle, who just shrugged. Ethan wasn't sure what to think. Was the old man talking about the same grove Knight Protector mentioned? Could he know the way to the Wellspring of Life?

Gramps continued, "Trees don't grow up in the prairie without lots of fresh water, so that's got to be the place yer lookin' fer."

Ethan's heart sang at the thought that they had a guide. "Really, you know the way?"

"Sure thing, youngster." Gramps nodded. "I know the bestest way there. Especially with the whole valley in a mess from the lakes bein' drained."

"So, you'll guide us to this grove?" Mother asked with raised eyebrows.

Gramps stroked his scraggly white beard for a moment. Ethan's heart skipped a beat, waiting for the answer.

TALK ABOUT A TIME WHEN YOUR HOPE WAS RENEWED.

PASSAGE QUESTIONS

Read the STORY PASSAGE and answer the following questions in your reading journal.

1. How did Gramps know where to find the grove they were looking for?
2. In the passage, what does "Ethan's heart sang" mean?
3. Do you think Gramps is going to help them?

Joke of the Day

I accidentally deleted an audiobook I was listening to with my kids.
Now I'll never hear the end of it!

DAY FIVE

READING & MEMORY VERSE

Read chapter eight in the book. Then, recite this week's memory verse aloud and complete the activity below. Include the coloring page and vocabulary puzzle with today's activities.

ACTIVITY: LAUREN'S SNOW GLOBE

MATERIALS

- Glass jar with lid (a lid with a rubber seal works best)
- Distilled water
- Glycerin or baby oil
- Small waterproof figurine
- Waterproof glue
- Glitter

Ratio: 3/4 cup water to 3 teaspoons glycerin to 2 teaspoons of glitter

INSTRUCTIONS

1. Take the lid off of your jar and glue whatever figurine you have chosen to the bottom of the inside of the lid. Make sure you center it first! Let the glue dry overnight.
2. Fill your jar with distilled water and add glycerin. The glycerin makes the glitter fall more slowly in the water. Don't overfill your globe. The water will rise when you insert your figure.
3. Next add glitter. Don't add too much or it will clump.
4. Put some glue around the edge of your lid and insert your figure into the globe.
5. Secure the lid tightly.
6. You may want to let the glue dry before flipping your globe upright.

LAUREN'S SNOW GLOBE POINTED THEM IN THE RIGHT DIRECTION. HOW DOES GOD POINT YOU IN THE RIGHT DIRECTION?

WEEK TWO
FRIEND OR FOE

Memory Verse:
"Wherewithal shall a young man cleanse his way? By taking heed thereto according to thy word. With my whole heart have I sought thee: O let me not wander from thy commandments. Thy word have I hid in mine heart, That I might not sin against thee."
—Psalm 119:9-11 KJV

LAUREN

VOCABULARY

WORD LIST

As part of your daily work this week, you'll need to use a dictionary and a thesaurus to look up definitions, synonyms, and antonyms for the words below.

ALBINO ELUSIVE PUNCTUATED
CUMBERSOME FURROWED SLAVERING

WORD SCRAMBLE

Rearrange each group of letters below to unscramble the words.

LESIUEV

__ __ __ __ __ __ __

UDAPTUTCNE

__ __ __ __ __ __ __ __ __ __

EROMEBMCSU

__ __ __ __ __ __ __ __ __ __

INOLBA

__ __ __ __ __ __

ERODURFW

__ __ __ __ __ __ __ __

VEIGRASNL

__ __ __ __ __ __ __ __ __

DAY ONE

MEMORY VERSE, VOCABULARY & READING

In your reading journal, copy this week's memory verse and vocabulary definitions. Then, read chapters nine and ten in the book.

STORY PASSAGE

What about the Wardens? How does any of this help us?"

"Tye, I'm not sure—"

"Enough of your explanations! Your Light may have helped me save my brother, but since then, it has done nothing but create trouble."

"What do you mean? You were under the control of the Darkness, we saved YOU with the Light," Lauren protested.

"Did you?" Tye's hard look told Lauren they were on treacherous ground. "To what end? Never-ending servitude to humans and their Light? Never to see my family or the woodlands of my youth again?"

Lauren was at a loss for words. How could she explain? The Savior said they might lose family and friends to embrace the Light. That the eternal blessings would outweigh the loss. But out here alone in the endless prairie, how could she help Tye see the Savior's glory?

HAVE YOU EVER GOTTEN INTO AN ARGUMENT OVER YOUR BELIEFS?

PASSAGE QUESTIONS

Read the STORY PASSAGE and answer the following questions in your reading journal.

1. What do you think Tye is the most upset about?
2. In the passage, what does "They were on treacherous ground" mean?
3. What are some clues that Tye doesn't want to listen to Lauren?

Joke of the Day

Which day of the week do potatoes dread the most?

Fry-day!

DAY TWO

MEMORY VERSE, VOCABULARY & READING

In your reading journal, copy this week's memory verse and list three synonyms for each vocabulary word. Then, read chapters eleven and twelve in the book.

STORY PASSAGE

"It's gone. We've looked everywhere," Jesse cried in frustration.
Ethan's jaw set hard. He was so mad at himself for letting Jesse have the snow globe. If he hadn't, it would be safely in the wagon. But was that even a safe place now?

"Now hold on. What are you sayin'?" Uncle put his hands on his hips.

The way Uncle's brows were furrowed made Ethan really not want to answer that question. Uncle must have figured that out because he demanded, "Well go on, out with it."

Ethan took a deep breath and explained, "I let Jesse have the snow globe as a little light to help him sleep. But it looks like the coyotes took it."

"Nope, not the coyotes." Gramps slammed his right fist into his left palm. "Them no-good egg-stealin' prairie dogs done took it."

Ethan raised his eyebrows. "What?"

"Lookie here, mixed amongst our tracks and the coyotes'—prairie-dog prints." Gramps pointed in the dust.

"Are you sure those weren't here before?" Uncle asked.

TALK ABOUT A DECISION THAT YOU HAD REGRETS ABOUT.

PASSAGE QUESTIONS

Read the STORY PASSAGE and answer the following questions in your reading journal.

1. In the passage, what does "Ethan's jaw set hard" mean?
2. How do Jesse and Ethan feel about losing the snow globe?
3. What is the theory that Gramps has about the snow globe's disappearance?

Joke of the Day

Why can't Jello cubes dance?
Because they're a bunch of squares!

DAY THREE

MEMORY VERSE, VOCABULARY & READING

In your reading journal, copy this week's memory verse and list three antonyms for each vocabulary word. Then, read chapters thirteen and fourteen in the book.

STORY PASSAGE

Mother pointed to Aiden's belt. "If anyone can repair this wagon and get us back to the others quickly, you can."

Aiden's chest swelled with pride at Mother's confidence, then deflated as he thought about Ethan, Uncle, and their new friends stranded somewhere far behind them. Were they OK? Did coyotes hurt them in the night? His confidence faltered under the weight of the responsibility.

Mother must have sensed this because she knelt in front of him. Tears brimming in her eyes, she said, "Aiden let's pray."

He closed his eyes and clasped his hands together, holding back his own tears.

Mother continued, "Father God, please give us wisdom beyond our understanding to reunite our family, and take us swiftly to the Wellspring of Life. Amen."

"Amen," Aiden repeated and gave Mother a mournful embrace. They sat there in the quiet for a moment, letting their tears come. Then Aiden slowly let go.

Mother wiped the tears from under his eyes. "You can do this, son."

He nodded. There had to be a way to save Father; he just had to think.

HAVE YOU EVER FELT YOUR CONFIDENCE RESTORED
AFTER PRAYING TO GOD?

PASSAGE QUESTIONS

Read the STORY PASSAGE and answer the following questions in your reading journal.

1. Why did Aiden's confidence falter when he thought of his family that was left behind?
2. Why do you think Mother decided to pray at that moment?
3. Do you think praying helped Aiden?

Joke of the Day

Why'd the cowboy adopt a Dachshund?
He wanted to get along little doggie!

DAY FOUR

MEMORY VERSE, VOCABULARY & READING

In your reading journal, copy this week's memory verse and draw a picture definition for each vocabulary word. Then, read chapters fifteen and sixteen in the book.

STORY PASSAGE

This time the hatchet went deep into the trunk and popped out two different pieces of wood, each about the size of a loaf of bread. "Perfect!" Aiden exclaimed.

"WOW! That was amazing," Logan replied, then offered the hatchet to Aiden. "These should go together."

Aiden held up his right hand palm out. "No, you keep yours. It takes a team."

"So we're a team?" Logan asked, eyebrows raised.

"Yah, like the Good Book says, 'as iron sharpens iron, one man sharpens another.'"

"That sounds good to me." Logan put his hatchet in his belt and picked up a log. Aiden did likewise, and they both ran back to the wagon. As they jogged up the beaten path, Aiden noticed how high the sun had gotten, it was nearly noon already, and they hadn't even started repairing the wagon. Would they be able to repair the wagon fast enough to save Father?

HOW IMPORTANT IS TEAMWORK?

PASSAGE QUESTIONS

Read the STORY PASSAGE and answer the following questions in your reading journal.

1. What did Logan do that gives a hint at his true character?
2. What does "as iron sharpens iron, one man sharpens another" mean?
3. Do you think having Logan as a friend helps Aiden's confidence?

Joke of the Day

Why is the Man on the Moon so fond of Darth Vader?
Because he also has a dark side!

DAY FIVE

READING & MEMORY VERSE

Read chapters seventeen thru nineteen in the book. Then, recite this week's memory verse aloud and complete the activity below. Include the coloring page and vocabulary puzzle with today's activities.

ACTIVITY: THE WAGON

MATERIALS

- A cardboard shoebox
- A thin dowel rod, cut into two equal pieces about an inch wider than the shoebox
- Cardboard to make wheels and seat
- Brown construction paper
- Scissors and glue
- Craft sticks (optional)

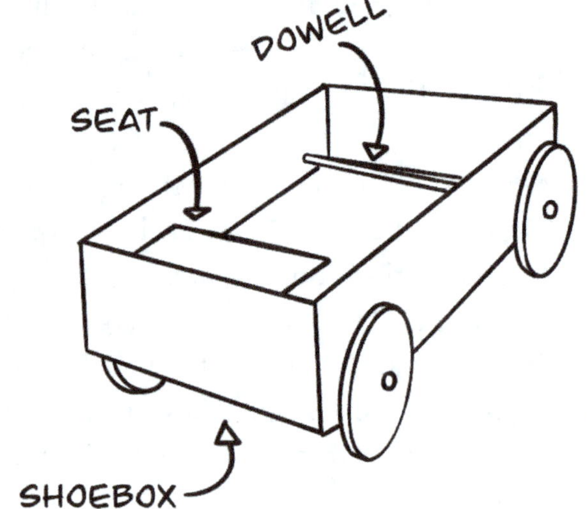

INSTRUCTIONS

1. Measure and cut the construction paper to cover the shoebox, and glue it in place.
2. On both sides of the long edge of the shoebox, poke two holes—one 1-2 inches from the front and the other 1-2 inches from the back. These are for the dowel rods, which will act as axles, so the holes need to line up across from each other.
3. Optional: Glue craft sticks to the sides of the box in a brick-like pattern for a realistic look. Be sure not to cover up the holes for the dowel rods.
4. Decide on the size of your wheels, then cut four identical circles out of the cardboard. Draw black spokes on them in an asterisk shape.
5. Put the dowel rods through the holes in the box.
6. You can either glue the wheels to the ends of the dowel rods or poke the dowel rods through the center of the wheels.
7. Cut a square out of the cardboard for the seat. Fold it in half and glue one half to the front top edge of the wagon. The edge left hanging will look like a seat.

WEEK THREE
CROSSFIRE

Memory Verse:
"Understanding is a wellspring of life unto him that hath
it: But the instruction of fools is folly."
—Proverbs 16:22 KJV

AIDEN

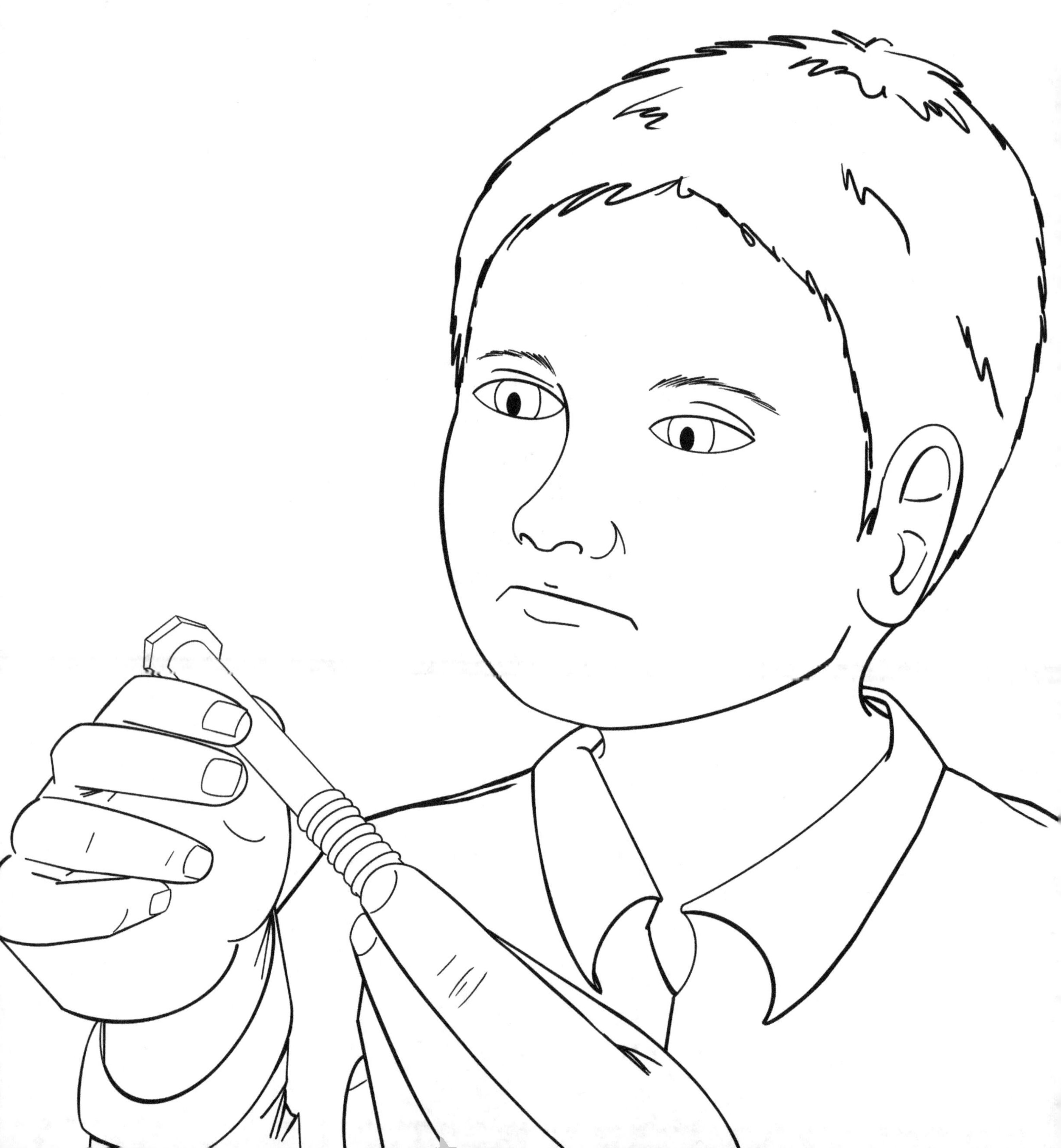

VOCABULARY

WORD LIST

As part of your daily work this week, you'll need to use a dictionary and a thesaurus to look up definitions, synonyms, and antonyms for the words below.

BAFFLED   FORMIDABLE   MANIACALLY
DEBRIS   FORTRESS   MONOTONOUS

MAZE

Help the kids find their way! Trace a path from the center of the maze to the outside.

DAY ONE

MEMORY VERSE, VOCABULARY & READING

In your reading journal, copy this week's memory verse and vocabulary definitions. Then, read chapters twenty and twenty-one in the book.

STORY PASSAGE

The coyotes must be close. Ethan gritted his teeth in a vain attempt to force the anxiety out of his body. His shield should keep them away, but what if it didn't work this time—the way his boots failed him?

Uncle continued, "If we can top the rise, we'll be able to see them comin', and if there's a sharp drop off, we can put that to our back."

"Well, let's get to it," Gramps said.

"Wait! What about Mama?" Ethan asked. "If we just run off down that path, how will she find us?"

"Can't worry about that now; we need to find a safe spot." Uncle picked up Ethan's pack in his free hand. "Ready your shield, and let's go!"

Ethan's face fell. He didn't want to lose this connection to his family. However, he knew there was no changing Uncle's mind.

"I know!" Jesse blurted out. "Mark the path with your sword. Cut arrows in the ground to show the way."

"With this grass bein' so dry, I'm afraid I'd start a fire." Uncle shook his head.

HOW CAN YOUR FAITH HELP YOU WITH ANXIETY?

PASSAGE QUESTIONS

Read the STORY PASSAGE and answer the following questions in your reading journal.

1. What is Ethan afraid of?
2. What is Jesse's plan for finding their way back?
3. Why is Uncle wary of Jesse's plan?

Joke of the Day

Why do tigers always beat cheetahs at hide and seek?
They've never been spotted!

DAY TWO

MEMORY VERSE, VOCABULARY & READING

In your reading journal, copy this week's memory verse and list three synonyms for each vocabulary word. Then, read chapters twenty-two thru twenty-four in the book.

STORY PASSAGE

The miles flew by, but Lauren soon realized the Censer was moving faster. She wanted to push their speed, but she knew that wouldn't help. They would be done for if they showed up spent from a mad race across the prairie.

Maybe the people at the settlement might prove a match for whatever minions of Darkness carried the Censer.

Two hours of carefully managing their speed brought them close enough to start to see the settlement in detail.

"Look! The Censer has stopped moving!" Tye pointed.

Sure enough, the Censer's smoke billowed at the top of the hill marked by the settlement. That flared Lauren's hope that the people at the farm might thwart the Darkness-minions' plan.

That hope vanished as she realized the fields below the settlement were on fire!

HOW CAN YOU MAKE GOOD CHOICES WHEN YOU ARE IMPATIENT?

PASSAGE QUESTIONS

Read the STORY PASSAGE and answer the following questions in your reading journal.

1. What is the benefit of regulating their speed instead of getting there as fast as possible?
2. Why have Tye and Lauren chosen the settlement as the place to try and catch the person with the Censer?
3. What problems do you foresee the fire causing?

Joke of the Day

What is it called if you steal someone's chicken finger?

Fowl play!

DAY THREE

MEMORY VERSE, VOCABULARY & READING

In your reading journal, copy this week's memory verse and list three antonyms for each vocabulary word. Then, read chapters twenty-five thru twenty-seven in the book.

STORY PASSAGE

"You keep saying you think this is the Wellspring of Life because it was on the snow globe. Do you know where that name comes from?"

"Well yah, the Good Book," Ethan replied

"The Good Book, yes that's right," Krystal replied. "What does the Good Book say about it?"

Ethan looked up at the ceiling and took a deep breath, then let it out. "I think it was something like protect your heart because it's the wellspring of life." He put his hand on the lantern symbol on his breastplate. "This armor it guards my heart. This place is a fortress, and that's the heart, right?" He pointed at the fountain.

Krystal seemed to crack a slight smile, and her hair took on a deep blue color. "That is very observant, but there is another verse you might know. 'Understanding is a wellspring of life unto him that hath it: but the instruction of fools is folly.'"

"Hey, I've heard that," Jesse exclaimed. "Gramps always says 'you can't teach a fool nothin'.'"

Krystal let out a sharp melody that Ethan thought might be a laugh.

WHY IS UNDERSTANDING THE WORD OF GOD SO IMPORTANT?

PASSAGE QUESTIONS

Read the STORY PASSAGE and answer the following questions in your reading journal.

1. Why does Ethan think the fountain in the room is the Wellspring of Life?
2. Why is Krystal quoting the Bible to the boys?
3. Do you think what Krystal tells Ethan and Jesse will be important knowledge to have?

Joke of the Day

What does a star get if it doesn't win?
A constellation prize!

DAY FOUR

MEMORY VERSE, VOCABULARY & READING

In your reading journal, copy this week's memory verse and draw a picture definition for each vocabulary word. Then, read chapters twenty-eight thru thirty in the book.

STORY PASSAGE

"Shut up, boy!" [Skull Crusher] cuffed Ethan in the mouth with his free hand and turned the cart to follow Lauren, only to end up face-to-face with Aiden driving the horse-drawn wagon straight at the cart!

"What!" The moose dodged back to the left in time to barely miss the wagon rolling over it.

Lauren wheeled Chance to chase after Skull Crusher.

Aiden kept driving straight forward, through the coyotes on one side of the prairie dog mound. A rainbow arced out of the wagon toward Tye's unconscious body. Sparkle Frog!

"Now you're in trouble!" Ethan hollered.

A whole murder of crows and the geese swooped in, driving the coyotes away.

Aiden pulled the wagon to a stop. "Uncle, help Gramps climb in!"

Lauren's heart leapt at the turn of events. They were going to put an end to Skull Crusher once and for all.

WHY IS IT EASIER TO FACE YOUR FEARS WHEN YOU HAVE SUPPORT?

PASSAGE QUESTIONS

Read the STORY PASSAGE and answer the following questions in your reading journal.

1. Why does Ethan tell Skull Crusher that he's in trouble?
2. Why is Lauren's hope suddenly renewed?
3. Do you think they will "put an end to Skull Crusher once and for all"?

Joke of the Day

What did the sandcastle say when it saw the tide come in?

Long time no sea!

DAY FIVE

READING & MEMORY VERSE

Read chapters thirty-one and thirty-two in the book. Then, recite this week's memory verse aloud and complete the activity below. Include the coloring page and vocabulary puzzle with today's activities.

ACTIVITY: KRYSTAL'S CRYSTALS

MATERIALS

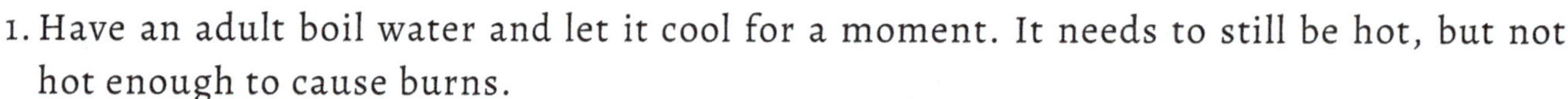

- Standard-size Mason jar
- Borax
- Hot water
- Craft stick
- Pipe cleaner
- Spoon

INSTRUCTIONS

1. Have an adult boil water and let it cool for a moment. It needs to still be hot, but not hot enough to cause burns.
2. Combine the water and borax in the Mason jar using a ratio of four parts water to one part borax. For a standard-size jar, use 2 cups hot water ½ cup Borax.
3. Stir! Make sure all the Borax is completely dissolved or the crystals will not form well.
4. Securely wrap one end of the pipe cleaner around the middle of the craft stick. Shape the rest of the pipe cleaner however you like.
5. Lay the craft stick across the opening of the jar so that the pipe cleaner is immersed in the water.
6. Wait 24-48 hours for crystals to form.

WHAT AMAZING THINGS HAVE YOU SEEN THAT GOD HAS CREATED?

Memory Verse:
"And the peace of God, which passeth all understanding, shall keep your hearts and minds through Christ Jesus."
—Philippians 4:7

ETHAN

VOCABULARY

WORD LIST

As part of your daily work this week, you'll need to use a dictionary and a thesaurus to look up definitions, synonyms, and antonyms for the words below.

CORDON

CREVASSE

GRIEVOUS

INCREDULOUS

STRONGHOLD

WAYLAYING

WORD SEARCH

Find and circle the hidden vocabulary words in the puzzle below. Words may appear up, down, forwards, backwards, or diagonally.

ALBINO

BAFFLED

BEFALL

CACOPHONY

CORDON

CREVASSE

CUMBERSOME

DEBRIS

ELUSIVE

EXASPERATED

FORMIDABLE

FORTRESS

FURROWED

GRIEVOUS

INCREDULOUS

IRONY

MANIACALLY

MONOTONOUS

PRONTO

PUNCTUATED

RESPITE

SLAVERING

STRONGHOLD

WAYLAYING

```
W I P H V Z B S S J R Y O D R Q X V E D A E D P M
S U E L B A D I M R O F N S E T I S C E L L E Q A
J S V B F Q C N F X B L U O E B S T Q W B U T J N
O L E F C U M B E R S O M E H A R E S O I S A G I
L T L R H P C V F M V J G T V P X I S R N I U S A
T E N T T U U I I E X D E Z A O M S R O V T L C
D B G O S R E P I F G J R W S Z G C W U H E C A A
Z J E A R O O R Y Z P C N P L Z E B A F M K N V L
F E M N M P G F I N C R E D U L O U S C I Y U E L
S U O N O T O N O M Y R D T Q C Y N V V O R P R Y
R E S P I T E I I G A D L O H G N O R T S M O I Q
W A Y L A Y I N G T O A X G G E H D M L K G X N N
W M N S S C B F E M P V L J T L V R S N S R X G Y
L L A F E B Y D Y P G Y H T I A H O H E J P O K E
R G D Z G V C E E K I J P E B X J C N L L J O H P
```

DAY ONE

MEMORY VERSE, VOCABULARY & READING

In your reading journal, copy this week's memory verse and vocabulary definitions. Then, read chapters thirty-three thru thirty-five in the book.

STORY PASSAGE

Tye whipped the end of the spear up and connected with his arm as he threw. The blow kicked the furball into a lazy arc right past the Master Warden's head. It came apart in flight and trailed yellow dust as it went. Lauren could almost see the Master Warden inhale it as little welts started to erupt all over his face.

"You are a stupid girl." Skull Crusher yelled. "You've killed your father to save a wretched human!"

A wave of horror went down Lauren's back as Master Warden began to gasp and claw at his face.

"Now!" Aiden cried as he slammed his hammer into the ground.

Logan followed up with a swing of the back of his axe onto Aiden's hammer. A wave of power fanned out from the strike, leveling the prairie grass, knocking most of the bison to their knees, and scattering the coyotes in front of the wagon. Logan hit it again, toppling the rest of the bison as Gramps kicked the horses into high gear.

Tye still had her hand loosely on Lauren's neck. She looked up at the giantess, hoping to see a sign that she was on Lauren's side. But Tye just stood there, dumbfounded with her mouth hanging open.

HOW DO YOU ASK FOR GOD'S HELP WHEN YOU SUFFER A LOSS?

PASSAGE QUESTIONS

Read the STORY PASSAGE and answer the following questions in your reading journal.

1. Why is the furball's dust so poisonous?
2. What does dumbfounded mean?
3. Why do you think Tye is frozen in place?

DAY TWO

MEMORY VERSE, VOCABULARY & READING

In your reading journal, copy this week's memory verse and list three synonyms for each vocabulary word. Then, read chapters thirty-six and thirty-seven in the book.

STORY PASSAGE

"Tye, please listen to me." Mother spoke slowly and softly, which scared Aiden more than when she had the sword out. If she was using her quiet voice, you just knew there was big trouble coming. "The only other Warden that knows the truth of Skull Crusher's betrayal is your father." She pointed her sword to where he lay in the wagon with his feet hanging out of the gate.

"Which is why it is my right to show this traitor Justice." Tye pointed the dagger at Mother.

"But that won't clear your name with the other Wardens." Mother slowly sheathed her sword. "It would be easy for Refi'Cul or a giant under the control of the Darkness to undermine your claims."

Mother stood motionless for a moment. Aiden held his breath as Tye seemed to be mulling over Mother's point. This was a lot more complicated than he thought.
Tye lowered her blade. "So, what would you have me do?"

"We'll restrain him and bring him with us." Mother stepped up to Tye. "Then in the presence of the Light, God willing, Skull Crusher will answer to your father in front of your people, clearing your name once and for all."

HAVE YOU EVER FELT LIKE DOING SOMETHING FOR REVENGE?

PASSAGE QUESTIONS

Read the STORY PASSAGE and answer the following questions in your reading journal.

1. What were Tye's plans for Skull Crusher?
2. Why does Tye feel she has the right to be the one to show justice to Skull Crusher?
3. How does Mother help Tye understand that there is a better way?

Joke of the Day

What school supply is always tired?
A knapsack!

DAY THREE

MEMORY VERSE, VOCABULARY & READING

In your reading journal, copy this week's memory verse and list three antonyms for each vocabulary word. Then, read chapter thirty-eight in the book.

STORY PASSAGE

Ethan pointed up the path. "So it wouldn't be long to go light the tower there. Isn't that what we're supposed to do, shine our light over the whole wide world?" He spread his arms out wide. "I promised the little girl I'd shine my light for her."

Deep down, Lauren knew Ethan was right. They couldn't let the Darkness continue to cover Zoura. So many other families were suffering.

Father cleared his throat as if to speak when a light splash caught everyone's attention.

Master Warden coughed and spoke weakly in a raspy voice, "Lord Refi'Cul means to trap you in Blooming Glen. He plans to make it a stronghold of giants and Steele Brothers for the Darkness." Tye ran to him, splashing through the pool, knelt, and hugged him fiercely.

What resolve Lauren had gained from Ethan's plea was only paper-thin, because it blew away at the thought of another battle.

Everyone watched as Father forced himself to his feet. He wobbled, and Mother came to his side. "Though my wounds are grievous, I do not regret the fight. The Darkness only wins when Light Bearers do nothing. We cannot allow that stronghold to stand."

HOW DO YOU SHINE YOUR LIGHT IN THE WORLD?

PASSAGE QUESTIONS

Read the STORY PASSAGE and answer the following questions in your reading journal.

1. Do you think the family should listen to Ethan even though he is a little boy?
2. How do you know that Master Warden is no longer loyal to Refi'Cul?
3. How important was it for Father to say what he did?

Joke of the Day

Have you read the book about hands?
It's a real page-turner!

DAY FOUR

MEMORY VERSE, VOCABULARY & READING

In your reading journal, copy this week's memory verse and draw a picture definition for each vocabulary word. Then, read chapter thirty-nine in the book.

STORY PASSAGE

The entire town was gathered around the spectacle, many of whom were wailing and weeping. The Mighty Mercenaries loyal to Garrison Master had created a cordon around the work site supported by the giants, and the Steele Brothers formed a tighter circle around Refi'Cul.

Journey Leader stood at the Steele Lord's side and asked, "Why this, my Lord? Surely there are better ways to destroy this monument? A fire would be easy enough."
Refi'Cul frowned. "Oh no, that would be too easy. Fires happen all the time. That sets no example to the people."

Refi'Cul waved his hand to the giants at the base of the tower, and they swung their mighty axes. "Having these so-called Light Bearers rip down this beacon of hope in front of the people will ensure they see the folly of their ways."

The sound of axes chopping into the tower punctuated his sentence.

"I see." Journey Leader rubbed his chin.

HOW DO YOU KEEP YOUR FAITH DURING DARK TIMES?

PASSAGE QUESTIONS

Read the STORY PASSAGE and answer the following questions in your reading journal.

1. What is Journey Leader confused about?
2. Why does Refi'Cul have the Light Bearers tear down the tower?
3. In the passage, what does the "folly of their ways" mean?

Joke of the Day

What did the bowler say when he was accused of cheating?

I was framed!

DAY FIVE

READING & MEMORY VERSE

Congratulations on finishing the book! Today, recite this week's memory verse aloud and complete the activity below. Include the coloring page and vocabulary puzzle with today's activities.

ACTIVITY: GROVE OF RIGHTEOUSNESS TERRARIUM

MATERIALS

- Container (fish tanks work well)
- Small pebbles or gravel
- Soil
- A few small plants
- Small animal figurines
- Small, shallow, clear plastic container

INSTRUCTIONS

1. Put a layer of pebbles or gravel about ½ inch deep into the bottom of the container.
2. In one corner, bury the plastic container up to the top edge and put in a little water. This will act as a small pool.
3. Next, add 2-3 inches of soil, depending on how tall your container is.
4. Gently brush off the roots of your plants, and place them into the container. Leave space between them. Then, cover the plant roots with soil and pat down the soil.
5. Water the plants, but not too much.
6. Decorate your terrarium as you wish. You can add animals, including cougars and bears like the ones in the story.

Tips: Plants like club moss and small ferns work well together in terrariums. Woodland and tropical plants do better if you seal the top (plastic wrap will do). Be sure to leave a small hole or two for circulation. Keep your terrarium in indirect sunlight and only water as needed (if soil is very dry or plants look like they are wilting).

CAN YOU THINK OF WAYS THAT TAKING CARE OF PLANTS IS SIMILAR TO GROWING YOUR FAITH IN THE LORD?

DEMOLISHING THE STRONGHOLD

WEEK ONE
DARKNESS

Memory Verse:
"For though we walk in the flesh, we do not war after the flesh: (for the weapons of our warfare are not carnal, but mighty through God to the pulling down of strong holds;)"
—2 Corinthians 10:3-4 KJV

VOCABULARY

WORD LIST

As part of your daily work this week, you'll need to use a dictionary and a thesaurus to look up definitions, synonyms, and antonyms for the words below.

BATTLEMENT   GARRISON   MALCONTENT
CALAMITY   GLYPHS   VENDETTA

SECRET MESSAGE

This week's vocabulary words have been used to form the message below, but it's been encrypted to keep it a secret. Determine which letter in the alphabet corresponds to each number to decode the message.

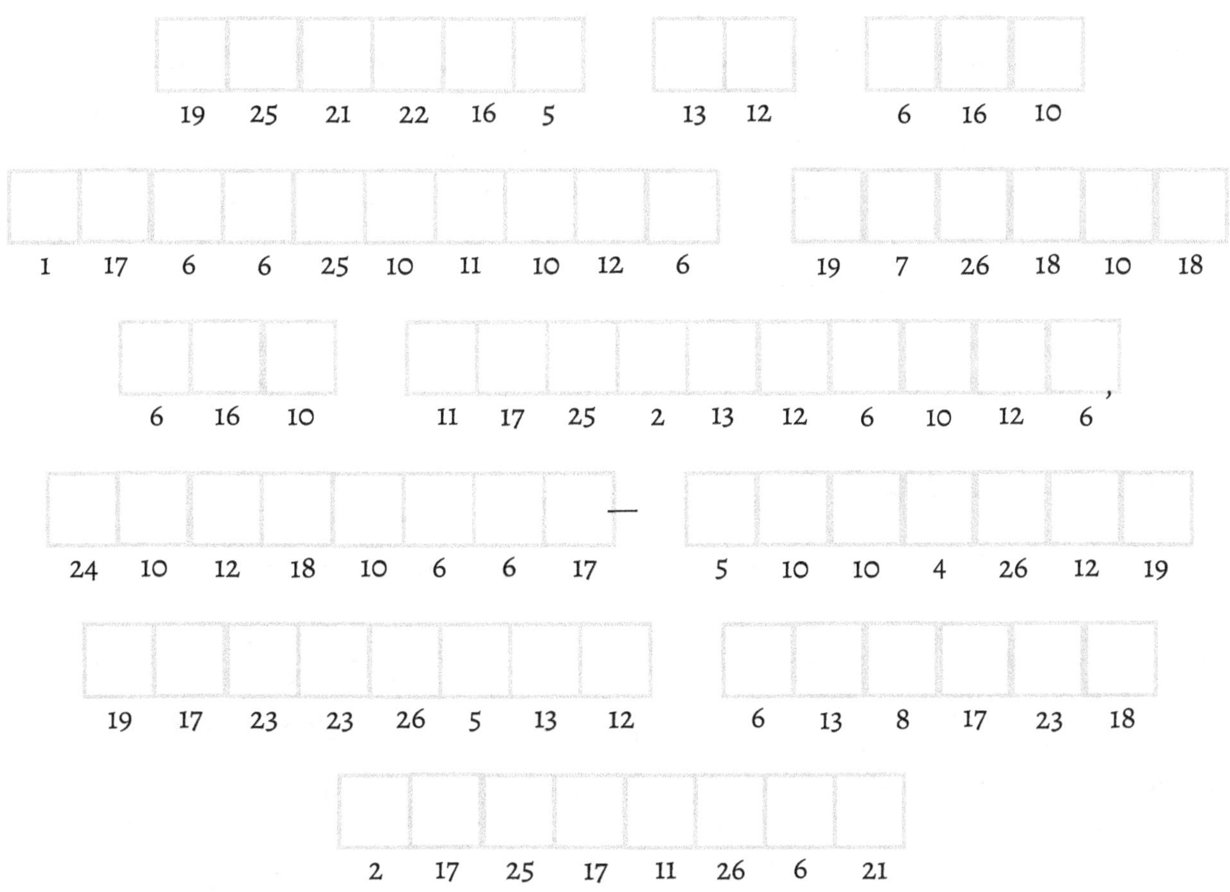

DAY ONE

MEMORY VERSE, VOCABULARY & READING

In your reading journal, copy this week's memory verse and vocabulary definitions. Then, read chapter one in the book.

STORY PASSAGE

Skull Crusher wondered where this was going. "My lord?"

"Journey Leader's reaction told me he may have a thing for Tye."

Skull Crusher did a double take. Refi'Cul was far more observant than he'd given the boy credit for. "I see."

Refi'Cul continued, "I need you to keep an eye on him. If there's an 'unfortunate accident,' I'll turn a blind eye."

Skull Crusher smiled wickedly. "As you wish, my lord."

Refi'Cul waved his hand in the direction of the moose. "Now get this animal out of here, refresh yourself, then report to the brig."

Skull Crusher didn't appreciate being dismissed condescendingly, especially without a mention of an attack on their foes. "But what of the enemy, my lord?"

The Steele Lord stared at the censer. "Bishop has that well in hand. When they come to light the tower—and they will—a calamity will befall them, I promise."

WHY DO LIES TEND TO LEAD TO MORE LIES?

PASSAGE QUESTIONS

Read the STORY PASSAGE and answer the following questions in your reading journal.

1. Why would Refi'Cul be worried that Journey Leader had "a thing for Tye"?
2. What did Refi'Cul mean when he said, "If there's an 'unfortunate accident,' I'll turn a blind eye"?
3. What kind of calamity do you think Bishop has planned?

DAY TWO

MEMORY VERSE, VOCABULARY & READING

In your reading journal, copy this week's memory verse and list three synonyms for each vocabulary word. Then, read chapter two in the book.

STORY PASSAGE

"If the guards are standing down to stay out of the rain and just waving people into the city, it's the perfect time to sneak in and light the tower, right?" Lauren stared into her mother's eyes. A moment passed between them where Mother's pride in Lauren for her courage and her fear over the path ahead was punctuated by a single tear forming in the corner of her eye.

Mother wiped her eyes. "So, who sneaks in? Are you suggesting we all load up in the wagon and walk into the city?"

"No, I don't think that would be wise." Lauren started hesitantly. She couldn't tell if Mother's scrutiny expected to find a fatal flaw to stop the plan or if she just wanted to understand. However, time was short, so Lauren had to push through her indecision. "We just want a few of us, who would 'make sense' to the guards, to enter. Is Blooming Glen the kind of place Wardens go to trade?"

Father nodded. "I saw a few from time to time."

"Yes, my people would occasionally trade there." Master Warden nodded in agreement. Lauren let out a brief sigh. Tye was an incredible fighter, and they were going to need her help if things went wrong.

HOW DOES GOD HELP YOU WITH DIFFICULT DECISIONS?

PASSAGE QUESTIONS

Read the STORY PASSAGE and answer the following questions in your reading journal.

1. Explain the moment that passed between Lauren and Mother.
2. In the passage, what does "Mother's scrutiny" mean?
3. Do you think Lauren's plan to sneak into Blooming Glen will work?

Joke of the Day

Why does Han Solo like gum?
Because it's chewy!

DAY THREE

MEMORY VERSE, VOCABULARY & READING

In your reading journal, copy this week's memory verse and list three antonyms for each vocabulary word. Then, read chapters three and four in the book.

STORY PASSAGE

Ethan glanced where the men had formed, and a Steele Brother stepped out of the building with his hood back. The others saluted him with fists to their chests. A shiver went down Ethan's spine when he recognized Refi'Cul!

The evil leader stepped to the front of the group and held up a black ram's horn that seemed to eat the light around it.

"Kids, it's a trap!" Mother called as she pointed to the other side of the courtyard, where a familiar black-clad giant stepped from the hall. "Run!" She pulled her sword, and it glowed with green firelight.

"Indeed!" Refi'Cul called, then put the horn to his lips and let out a blast that shook Ethan to his bones.

Suddenly the smoke over the censer filled with tendrils of red and turned into a cyclone of crimson and black smoke. From its midst formed the wings of a gigantic dragon made of smoke, and the Bishop stepped out of the fumes swirling at the base of the censer.

"Resistance is futile," Bishop said. "Zoura is now ours."

WHAT DO YOU DO WHEN YOUR PLANS GET RUINED?

PASSAGE QUESTIONS

Read the STORY PASSAGE and answer the following questions in your reading journal.

1. In the passage, what does "seemed to eat the light around it" mean?
2. Who did Mother see on the other side of the courtyard?
3. What does "resistance is futile" mean?

Joke of the Day

What does a tightrope walker have in the mornings?

A balanced breakfast!

DAY FOUR

MEMORY VERSE, VOCABULARY & READING

In your reading journal, copy this week's memory verse and draw a picture definition for each vocabulary word. Then, read chapters five and six in the book.

STORY PASSAGE

Where the smoky breath hit her exposed skin, it felt like she'd been whipped with stinging nettle. However, it seemed her armor had protected her head from the foul fumes. Without it, she knew either slamming her head into the wall or the smoke itself would have knocked her unconscious.

She'd managed to keep hold of her sword, which made it awkward as she tried to stand. Tendrils of black ink surrounded her, and her movements felt like they were being slowed by the presence of thick cobwebs. The smoke blocked sight of the courtyard and the forces advancing toward them. She felt like she'd fallen into an abyss, and despair began to creep in.

The familiar green light of Mother's sword erupted to her left. Uncle's fiery sword ignited as he gained his feet. It pushed back the dark smoke around them.

Despite the beating they took from the dragon's blast, their faith remained strong.

"God, I believe, help me with my unbelief," Tye whispered as she struggled to maintain the grip on her sword and stood. The stinging nettle feeling on the back of her sword hand and fingers washed away into pleasant heat, and her blade took on a pale glow.

TALK ABOUT A TIME WHEN GOD HELPED YOU WITH YOUR UNBELIEF.

PASSAGE QUESTIONS

Read the STORY PASSAGE and answer the following questions in your reading journal.

1. How did the smoke from Calamitous Drake make Tye feel?
2. How did the Armor of God help Tye?
3. What happened after Tye prayed?

Joke of the Day

Why did the little bird get in trouble at school?

He got caught tweeting on a test!

DAY FIVE

READING & MEMORY VERSE

Read chapter seven in the book. Then, recite this week's memory verse aloud and complete the activity below. Include the coloring page and vocabulary puzzle with today's activities.

ACTIVITY: CALAMITOUS DRAKE

MATERIALS

- Latex ballon
- Plastic grocery bag and black marker or black tissue paper (to make the dragon)
- Scissors

INSTRUCTIONS

1. Draw the shape of Calamitous Drake onto the grocery bag or tissue paper. If you're using the bag, color the dragon in, so it is all black. Let the marker dry well.
2. Cut out your dragon.
3. Blow up the balloon and tie it. Then, hold it by the tied end and rub it on someone's hair until their hair is standing up.
4. At the same time someone is rubbing the balloon, have someone rub the dragon on someone else's head until it wants to cling to your hand.
5. Hold your balloon out in front of you, then drop your dragon over the top of the balloon. The dragon will want to cling to your hand, but peel it off as quickly as possible.
6. If you do this right, the dragon will hover over your balloon, just like in the story! The balloon should push the Calamitous Drake away due to the static electricity.

TALK ABOUT HOW GOD HELPS YOU PUSH THE DARKNESS AWAY.

WEEK TWO
FAITH

Memory Verse:
*"The LORD is my light and my salvation;
whom shall I fear? The LORD is the strength of my life;
of whom shall I be afraid?"*
—Psalm 27:1 KJV

AIDEN

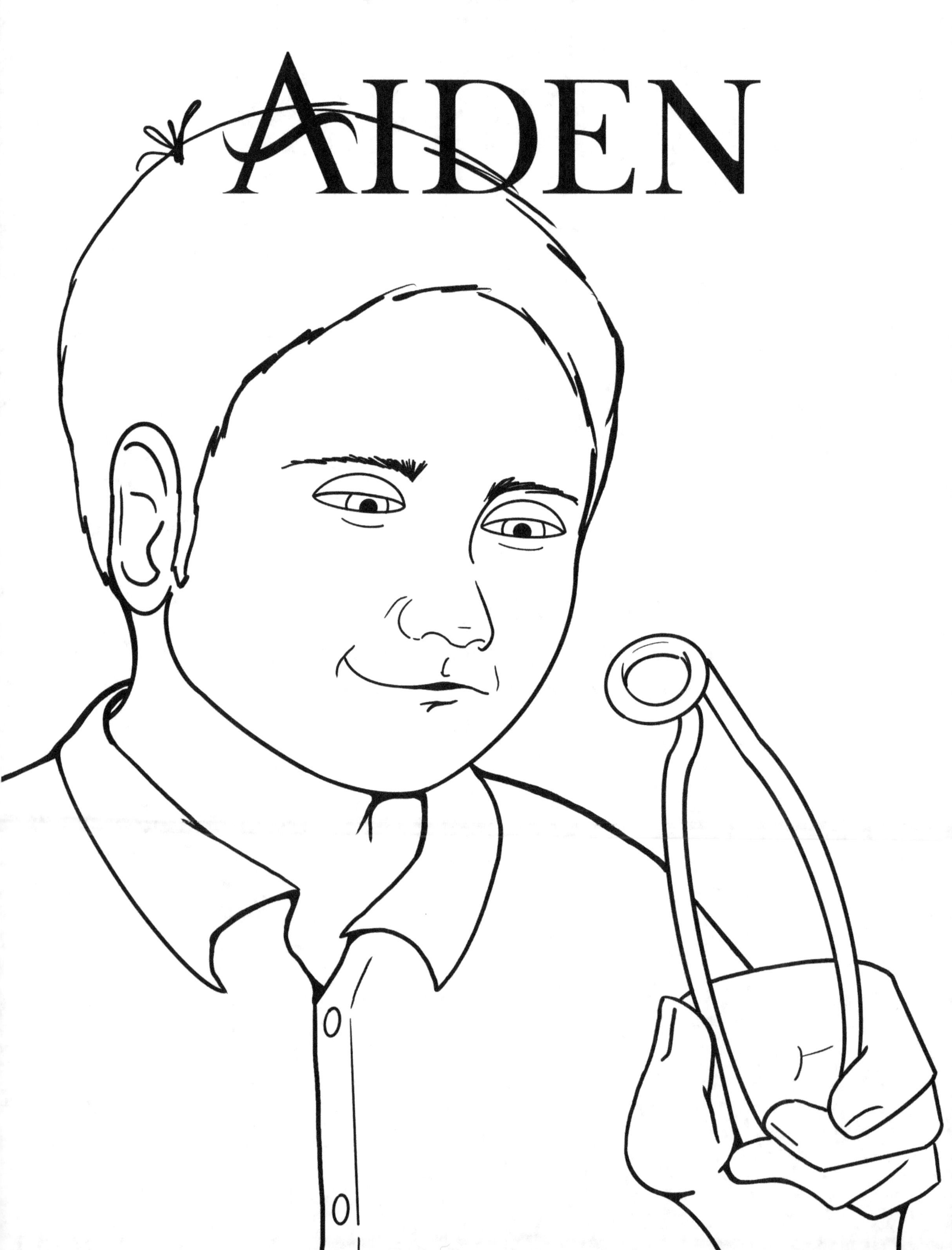

VOCABULARY

WORD LIST

As part of your daily work this week, you'll need to use a dictionary and a thesaurus to look up definitions, synonyms, and antonyms for the words below.

ALTERCATION   DENIZENS   INGOTS
CRESTFALLEN   FIBROUS   PARLAY

WORD SCRAMBLE

Rearrange each group of letters below to unscramble the words.

ALARPY

—— —— —— —— —— ——

LEFRANCLTES

—— —— —— —— —— —— —— —— —— —— ——

ATTRALECION

—— —— —— —— —— —— —— —— —— —— ——

OSGINT

—— —— —— —— —— ——

SINNEZED

—— —— —— —— —— —— —— ——

ISOFBUR

—— —— —— —— —— —— ——

DAY ONE

MEMORY VERSE, VOCABULARY & READING

In your reading journal, copy this week's memory verse and vocabulary definitions. Then, read chapters eight and nine in the book.

STORY PASSAGE

"Every minute they go unchecked, they dig their claws deeper into my people's lands."

"I want to save our people and have our loved ones returned to us as much as you do." Father seemed to catch Mitchell's attention. "All our loved ones, including your father, Mitchell. But we need a weapon to defeat this dragon if we have any hope of demolishing this stronghold of evil."

"Makes sense to me!" Gramps stamped his walking stick on the ground.

Master Warden deflated. "If it's the only way."

"Daddy! Pray!" Ethan blurted out.

Father cocked his head, eyes wide.

Ethan continued, "Knight protector said if you don't know what to do, you should pray, and the small voice will tell you."

Father let out a slight chuckle. "Wisdom from the mouth of babes."

"Hey! I'm no baby," Ethan retorted.

"It's a saying, son. You are right. We should pray."

TALK ABOUT A TIME WHEN YOU PRAYED FOR GUIDANCE.

PASSAGE QUESTIONS

Read the STORY PASSAGE and answer the following questions in your reading journal.

1. Why is Master Warden so impatient?
2. What does Father say is needed to defeat the dragon?
3. What does the saying "wisdom from the mouth of babes" mean?

> **Joke of the Day**
>
> Why did Mickey Mouse ride Space Mountain?
> He was looking for Pluto!

DAY TWO

MEMORY VERSE, VOCABULARY & READING

In your reading journal, copy this week's memory verse and list three synonyms for each vocabulary word. Then, read chapters ten and eleven in the book.

STORY PASSAGE

Refi'Cul felt a huge smile of appreciation crack his lips. Now it made sense. Bishop wanted her to see there was no way out for her family. That an overwhelming force was coming, and her only out was to make them surrender. Bishop was more shrewd than a serpent.

The mother sat up a little straighter. "You have no idea what waits for you in those woods because your false light has told you nothing!" She spat on the ground. "Your mercenaries and militia will find out soon enough that you've sent them to their doom. I'll not save you from it by telling our people to stand down."

Master at Arms's pudgy face turned white, and he took a step back from her. But Mercenary Captain seemed to stand a little straighter. "Look woman! You're the one behind bars right now because of Lord Refi'Cul's trap. Pretty sure we can handle a handful of kids and whatever nonsense they might be able to come up with."

"Quite right, Captain, quite right." Bishop encouraged. The anxiety on the Master at Arms's face subsided. Maybe the shopkeeper-turned-warrior would be useful after all?

HOW DOES GOD HELP YOU SHOW STRENGTH WHEN YOU FEEL WEAK?

PASSAGE QUESTIONS

Read the STORY PASSAGE and answer the following questions in your reading journal.

1. What is Bishop planning to have the Mercenaries do?
2. Why does Bishop have the meeting in the jail?
3. What is Mother's reaction to Bishop's suggestion that she have her family surrender?

DAY THREE

MEMORY VERSE, VOCABULARY & READING

In your reading journal, copy this week's memory verse and list three antonyms for each vocabulary word. Then, read chapters twelve and thirteen in the book.

STORY PASSAGE

"Aiden, are you sure what building we're going to?"

"Yah." Aiden nodded. "The forge had the biggest smokestack in the city."

Lauren gulped down a pang of nausea and continued, "Do you think the birds would work together?"

Aiden's eyes got big. "Maybe. What do you have in mind?"

"Daddy Duck does a good job of shining light on things." Lauren paused to take another slow deep breath. "So do you think if he shined his light on the smokestack, the other birds would follow?"

"That's not a bad idea," Aiden replied. "See, Father knew you had to be the leader."

The corner of her mouth turned up unexpectedly at his praise but quickly fell to a grimace as she choked down another bout of sickness.

"Lauren, you're looking really green," Mitchell commented as he reached into his pocket. Now he was making fun of her. She hated that they had to bring him along.

He reached his arm toward Aiden without moving from the corner, holding a white cloth bag just slightly bigger than a pint canning jar. "Pass this to Lauren."

HAS YOUR FIRST IMPRESSION OF SOMEONE TURNED OUT TO BE WRONG?

PASSAGE QUESTIONS

Read the STORY PASSAGE and answer the following questions in your reading journal.

1. What is Lauren's plan to land the balloon?
2. Do you think her plan will work well?
3. Lauren doesn't seem to care for Mitchell. Do you think her opinion will change?

Joke of the Day

Why doesn't Superman need a boss?
He already has super vision!

DAY FOUR

MEMORY VERSE, VOCABULARY & READING

In your reading journal, copy this week's memory verse and draw a picture definition for each vocabulary word. Then, read chapters fourteen thru sixteen in the book.

STORY PASSAGE

Father had every tool you could imagine. Even a massive press hung from the ceiling, ready to flatten just about anything on the vice. He'd ask Father to show him how to use it properly someday.

But the tools weren't the real difference. Not having Master Warden's disapproving stare boring into him helped him relax and do the job. Father was right. He was meant to do this work.

Aiden carefully pulled the ring out of the fire. It seemed hot enough he might bend it out of round if he wasn't careful. So he took the greatest care with the tongs. He held it like a baby chick.

When he set the ring on the pommel of the dagger, it fit just a little too loosely, and he wondered if he'd chosen the wrong one. But then he remembered that the metal expanded when it got hot, so he set to tap it into place with his hammer. Once he seated it properly, he stood back and watched it cool. As the color faded from bright orange to red, the gem in the center began to slowly glow. By the time the metal faded to purple, the gem glowed brightly.

HOW DOES GOD HELP YOU RELAX WHEN YOU ARE DOING A TASK?

PASSAGE QUESTIONS

Read the STORY PASSAGE and answer the following questions in your reading journal.

1. What made the most difference in helping Aiden to relax and realize he was meant to do the same type of work as Father?
2. Why do you think that the gem glowed brightly?

Joke of the Day

Why did the M&M go to space?
It wanted to visit the Milky Way!

DAY FIVE

READING & MEMORY VERSE

Read chapters seventeen and eighteen in the book. Then, recite this week's memory verse aloud and complete the activity below. Include the coloring page and vocabulary puzzle with today's activities.

ACTIVITY: MITCHELL'S HOT AIR BALLOON

MATERIALS

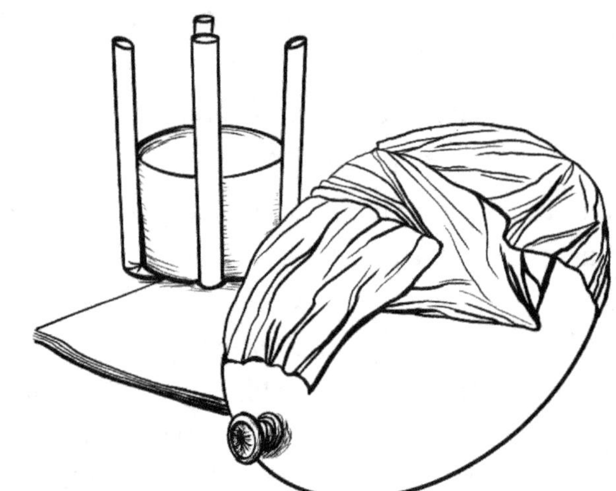

- A balloon
- Tissue paper (white and colored)
- 4 long straws
- Paper cup (for the hot air balloon)
- School glue and hot glue
- Paintbrush
- Water

INSTRUCTIONS

1. Cut your tissue paper into 1 1/2 inch squares. You will need five sheets of white tissue to every sheet of colored tissue paper.
2. Mix ½ cup water with ½ cup school glue. Blow up your balloon. Paint glue on the balloon and attach the white tissue paper to iy, then paint over the tissue paper with glue. Leave about an inch around the tie of the balloon without glue so you will be able to pop it later. Do three layers of white tissue paper and let dry overnight.
3. Repeat the next day with two layers of white tissue paper and one layer of colored tissue paper on the top. You can add more layers to make your balloon sturdier.
4. Use the hot glue gun to glue the four straws to the bottom of the paper cup (hot air balloon basket). Glue them from each corner coming up and out at an angle. Your balloon will sit in the straws.
5. When the balloon is dry, pop the balloon on the inside and it should come out. Sit the balloon in between the four straws however you like, then hot glue the straws to the outside of the balloon.

WEEK THREE
CALL TO ARMS

Memory Verse:
"Woe unto them that call evil good, and good evil; that put darkness for light, and light for darkness; that put bitter for sweet, and sweet for bitter!"
—Isaiah 5:20 KJV

ETHAN

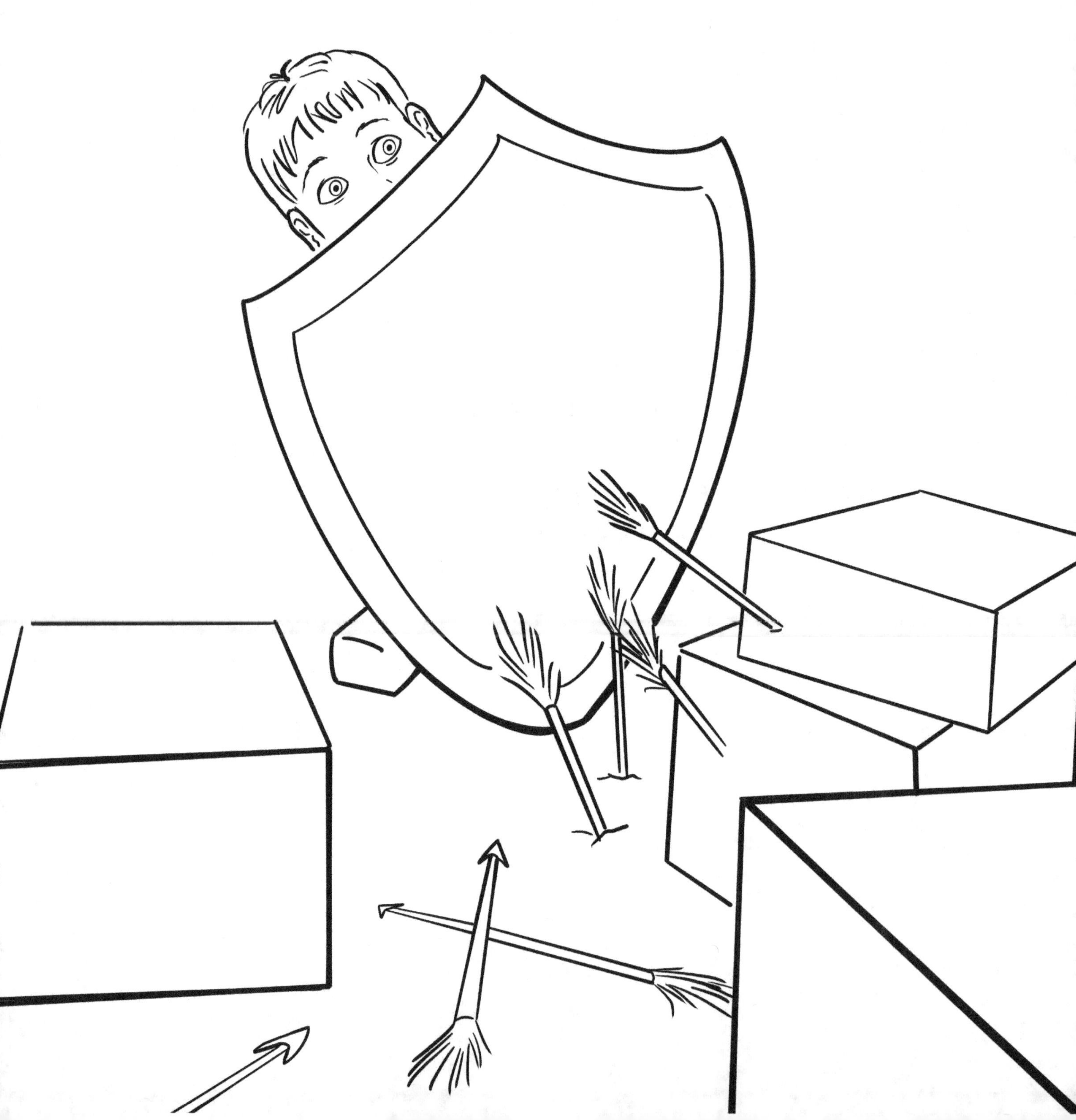

VOCABULARY

WORD LIST

As part of your daily work this week, you'll need to use a dictionary and a thesaurus to look up definitions, synonyms, and antonyms for the words below.

COMPATRIOTS   IMPENDING   PARAPET
EMBOLDENED   MELEE   PROFFERING

MAZE

Help the kids penetrate the stronghold! Trace a path through the maze.

DAY ONE

MEMORY VERSE, VOCABULARY & READING

In your reading journal, copy this week's memory verse and vocabulary definitions. Then, read chapters nineteen thru twenty-one in the book.

STORY PASSAGE

"Enough of this!" a man in a complete set of the armor of God called from the edge of the pool.

Ethan's heart leapt in his chest. Was that Knight Protector? The bears stopped their pursuit of the mercenaries and started to form a wall, protecting Master Warden. "By the Code of the Mighty Mercenaries, I command you to stand down!"

The retreating mercenaries used this as an opportunity to regroup with their leader. "Who do you think you are trying to command the Mighty Mercenaries? Archers dispense with that fool, then the bears!"

"I'm the father of a boy who needs a good spanking!"

Ethan cracked a smile but then thought about it for a second. If the man in armor was Knight Protector, his son had turned to the Darkness. Ethan's smile fell at the thought. That must hurt Knight Protector terribly.

In answer to Ethan's suspicions, the man in the armor of God took his helmet off to reveal Knight Protector.

HAVE YOU EVER HAD A FAMILY MEMBER WHO WAS AFFECTED BY THE DARKNESS OF THE WORLD?

PASSAGE QUESTIONS

Read the STORY PASSAGE and answer the following questions in your reading journal.

1. How did Ethan feel when the man in the armor of God showed up?
2. Why did Ethan change how he felt about the man when he said that Mercenary Leader needed a good spanking?
3. Who did the man in the armor of God turn out to be?

Joke of the Day

Why did the farmer bury cash in his field?

He wanted to make it rich!

DAY TWO

MEMORY VERSE, VOCABULARY & READING

In your reading journal, copy this week's memory verse and list three synonyms for each vocabulary word. Then, read chapters twenty-two thru twenty-four in the book.

STORY PASSAGE

"Turmeric, some turmeric tea would definitely hit the spot for our wounded warden," La'Ren's mother called.

"Oh, of course, I can be back with that in a jiffy." She paused for a moment and cocked her head. "Actually, I'll come back in about half an hour to get your plates, that wouldn't be suspicious, and I'll let you know if, between now and then, I run into any of these Wolf Brothers."

"Thank you so much," Tye replied as the woman turned to leave. Before her foot crossed the doorway, Uncle called, "This venison is sure some fine dining, best I ever had. Any chance you can bring back an equally high-dollar toothpick to go with them?" He winked at her.

"I'll see what I can do." She blushed as she pulled the door shut behind her.

Tye couldn't help but smile. Even in the heart of such a desperate situation, Uncle still thought with his stomach. Her stomach growled at her, so maybe he had the right idea. She began to devour the food in the hopes of blocking out all thoughts of becoming the Skull Crusher's bride.

PASSAGE QUESTIONS

Read the STORY PASSAGE and answer the following questions in your reading journal.

1. Why do you think the woman is helping Tye and the others?
2. Why do you think Uncle asked the woman for a toothpick?
3. Do you think the woman is a good person? Why?

> **Joke of the Day**
>
> What do Vikings play on a long journey?
> Cards, because they have a deck!

DAY THREE

MEMORY VERSE, VOCABULARY & READING

In your reading journal, copy this week's memory verse and list three antonyms for each vocabulary word. Then, read chapters twenty-five and twenty-six in the book.

STORY PASSAGE

The words "I'm gonna let it shine" hung in the air as a group of people rounded the corner, carrying sledgehammers, pickaxes, garden rakes, and little lanterns. They carried the light before them, and it began to cut through the smoke of the dwindling fires, pushing it back as if the light were at war with the smoke.

Dozens of people, young, old, men, women, and even a few children, poured into the street in front of the foundry. The giants grabbed up their wounded comrades and started off in the opposite direction of the balloon, only to see more light coming from there, so they rushed off away from the gathering mobs where Daddy Duck circled overhead, blocking the Steele Brothers from following the giants with his Light.

Sensing their doom, the Steele Brothers began to retreat into the foundry. Lauren picked off a few as they darted into the building, but at least two dozen found refuge in the building they had set on fire.

Lauren wondered for a moment if they were hoping the burning building might provide the strength and possibly smoke needed to escape. She didn't wonder long because the townsfolk started a bucket brigade, dumping water on the fire and quickly extinguishing it.

WHY IS THE LIGHT SO MUCH STRONGER WHEN WE SHINE IT TOGETHER?

PASSAGE QUESTIONS

Read the STORY PASSAGE and answer the following questions in your reading journal.

1. How did you feel when you read that the townspeople arrived with the Light?
2. Why did the Steele Brothers run into the foundry?
3. What is a bucket brigade?

Joke of the Day

Why should you be nice to pies?
You don't want to hurt their fillings!

DAY FOUR

MEMORY VERSE, VOCABULARY & READING

In your reading journal, copy this week's memory verse and draw a picture definition for each vocabulary word. Then, read chapters twenty-seven and twenty-eight in the book.

STORY PASSAGE

"Mitchell, quick! Put Aiden's helmet on!"

"What?" He blurted.

Aiden was just as confused as Mitchell. He had hoped to put the helmet on because it might help with his hurting face. What was she thinking?

"Just do it!" Lauren called back as she struggled to a knee.

Mitchell bobbled the helmet but managed to get control and plop it on his head as the smoke engulfed them. The force knocked them all flat on the ground. Aiden could see a slight blueish glow emanating from his breastplate that seemed to cover his body. In the whirling blast, he vaguely caught sight of a similar light covering the others. He let out a sigh of relief that they were all safe. Lauren was right to give Mitchell the helmet after all. They all needed the armor to protect them from the smoke, but the force of the blast was still no joke.

Logan must have been thinking the same thing as the smoke rolled passed them. "This is what those giants must have felt like when we were blasting them."

TALK ABOUT HOW USING THE ARMOR OF GOD WEAKENS THE DARKNESS.

PASSAGE QUESTIONS

Read the STORY PASSAGE and answer the following questions in your reading journal.

1. Why does Lauren insist that Mitchell put on Aiden's helmet?
2. What happens when the dragon's smoke engulfs them?
3. What does Logan think about the force of the dragon's blast?

Joke of the Day

Why doesn't the Queen of Hearts go to the Mad Hatter's tea parties?
He doesn't serve royal-tea!

DAY FIVE

READING & MEMORY VERSE

Read chapters twenty-nine thru thirty-one in the book. Then, recite this week's memory verse aloud and complete the activity below. Include the coloring page and vocabulary puzzle with today's activities.

ACTIVITY: JEWLIES

MATERIALS

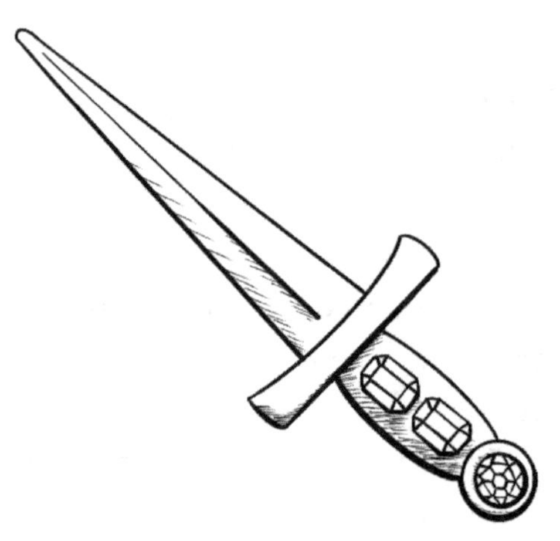

- White air-dry clay or Model Magic clay
- Small assorted craft jewels
- Tweezers
- Tempera paint and small brushes
- Self-adhesive magnets (optional)

INSTRUCTIONS

1. Mold the clay into whatever you like. For example, you could recreate Lauren's spear or Mother's dagger.
2. Then, use the tweezers and pretend that you are an artificer like Father and Aiden. Take great care and place the jewels carefully where you need them to go.
3. Let the clay dry, then you can paint your creations however you like.
4. Optional: When the paint is dry, attach a magnet to the back! Make more for your friends!

HOW HAVE YOU LEARNED TO USE THE ARMOR OF GOD?

WEEK FOUR
LIGHT

Memory Verse:
"Then spake Jesus again unto them, saying, I am the light of the world: he that followeth me shall not walk in darkness, but shall have the light of life."
—John 8:12 KJV

LAUREN

VOCABULARY

WORD LIST

As part of your daily work this week, you'll need to use a dictionary and a thesaurus to look up definitions, synonyms, and antonyms for the words below.

BANTER   FEROCITY   TACTICAL
EMBLEM   SCABBARD   USURP

WORD SEARCH

Find and circle the hidden vocabulary words in the puzzle below. Words may appear up, down, forwards, backwards, or diagonally.

ALTERCATION	DENIZENS	GLYPHS	PARLAY
BANTER	EMBLEM	IMPENDING	PROFFERING
BATTLEMENT	EMBOLDENED	INGOTS	SCABBARD
CALAMITY	FEROCITY	MALCONTENT	TACTICAL
COMPATRIOTS	FIBROUS	MELEE	USURP
CRESTFALLEN	GARRISON	PARAPET	VENDETTA

```
D X T C I N G O T S A G J L C I R Z M K W N M R X
P R O F F E R I N G Y U X M P D R W F Y Z B V V P
A S G F E L Q C M C G H C B A G E E V J G Z N E A
N G T E E E D X R S A E P O A L A N M P N G O N R
H P F L M R A I A E V L O D M T C R I B M J Q D L
F H A I J B O J S O S N A H I P T O R Z L G O E A
I S C R N I O C D G P T X M X M A L N I E E S T Y
B C T K A L O L I U P T F M I H P T E T S N M T K
R A A Q G P A W D T Q L F A I T D E R M E O S A S
O B C K L U E K U E Y K O X L F Y J N I E N N B F
U B T H Y A D T D K N O I C Q L F C S D O N T U T
S A I J P L D X V Y Y E L W D W E D S K I T T S V
M R C F H S F N M T L H D M S Q G N E S I N S U Z
Q D A G S F V N G E M A L T E R C A T I O N G R X
Q U L I M E L E E C G T V X I Z B A N T E R R P L
```

DAY ONE

MEMORY VERSE, VOCABULARY & READING

In your reading journal, copy this week's memory verse and vocabulary definitions. Then, read chapters thirty-two and thirty-three in the book.

STORY PASSAGE

When Mother was pulled from her cell, she recovered and stared into Tye's eyes. Somehow, they reflected a light as bright as the sun. The tiny woman smiled a kind smile, put her hands together and nodded down in prayer. A refreshing warmth came over Tye.

The militia jerked Mother out the door and started on Uncle's bonds. Through the pounding Tye thought of Mother's quiet defiance. Despite being surrounded by warriors, chains, and the fall of hammers, this woman truly believed God would protect her and her family—and Tye was part of her family.

Tye put her own hands together and bowed. God, I believe, help my unbelief. Please show me the way to save our family.

When she looked up from her prayers, she didn't understand why they had saved her for last. As the bride, she thought they might give her priority and treat her more gently, but they were just as rough with her as the others. She thought to say something, then thought better of it. Better to save her energy for an opportunity to break free if it came.

DO YOU KNOW SOMEONE WHO SEEMS TO HAVE UNSHAKABLE FAITH?

PASSAGE QUESTIONS

Read the STORY PASSAGE and answer the following questions in your reading journal.

1. How does Mother reassure and comfort Tye?
2. How does Tye show her faith?
3. Why do you think the militia treated Tye so roughly even though she was to be the bride?

Joke of the Day

Why was the cat so small?
It only drank condensed milk!

DAY TWO

MEMORY VERSE, VOCABULARY & READING

In your reading journal, copy this week's memory verse and list three synonyms for each vocabulary word. Then, read chapters thirty-four thru thirty-six in the book.

STORY PASSAGE

In the distance, the dragon rose out of the city and hovered for just a moment to rain black smoke. Lauren lost sight of it in the haze it created and the dark of the night sky. Her blood turned to ice as her deepest fears about attacking at night were realized. How could she hit a target she couldn't see?

Iron Sister turned to Lauren. "We ride?"

The gem on Lauren's spear glittered internally, and the spear's power resonated in her hand, driving back the fear. If God was for them even the dragon would not stand against them.

Lauren nodded toward Iron Sister. "Yes! Let's destroy that abomination once and for all. Charge, Chance! Charge," she called, and the pony responded.

Iron Sister's bison and the two bears fell in behind her.

As they closed with the west flank, Lauren could tell the firepots had done their job putting the enemy in complete disarray. Lauren wondered why the enemy hadn't used spears or bows to attack them more directly. The dragon answered her question by breaking through the smoke at the edge of the city and attacking their unprotected flank with its breath.

HOW DO YOU REMEMBER THAT GOD IS FOR YOU WHEN YOU ARE AFRAID?

PASSAGE QUESTIONS

Read the STORY PASSAGE and answer the following questions in your reading journal.

1. Why was Lauren afraid of attacking the dragon at night?
2. What calmed Lauren's fears?
3. Why wasn't the enemy fighting with spears or bows?

DAY THREE

MEMORY VERSE, VOCABULARY & READING

In your reading journal, copy this week's memory verse and list three antonyms for each vocabulary word. Then, read chapters thirty-seven thru forty-one in the book.

STORY PASSAGE

"No! You'll not get away again!" Lauren yelled as she let her spear fly. It left a white streak behind it as it lanced through the air, this time connecting with the dragon, causing it to disappear in a shower of white sparks.

"Sissy, you came!" Ethan's voice rang out overhead and she realized his shield was shining Light in the tower. A broad smile broke out as her spear returned to her hand and Bishop came into view.

She readied to throw, when Bishop yelled, "Not so fast!" as he grabbed Mitchell and pulled him close, threatening him with a wicked knife at his throat. "You may have defeated my dragon, but I'll be walking out that front gate unharmed." The Steele Brothers near Bishop moved to provide protection for him while in the distance two dozen more carrying doors for shields closed in.

The sound of thunder split the air, and streaks of lightning crisscrossed the sky. Lauren knew her spear could end this once and for all, but should she risk Mitchell getting hurt in the process?

HOW DO YOU DECIDE WHAT RISKS TO TAKE?

PASSAGE QUESTIONS

Read the STORY PASSAGE and answer the following questions in your reading journal.

1. What happens to Calamitous Drake?
2. What does Bishop do to try to ensure his escape?
3. Do you think Lauren will risk throwing her spear while Bishop holds Mitchell?

Joke of the Day

Which video game does Charlie Brown play?
Minecraft, because he's a block head.

DAY FOUR

MEMORY VERSE, VOCABULARY & READING

In your reading journal, copy this week's memory verse and draw a picture definition for each vocabulary word. Then, read the chapter forty-two and forty-three in the book.

STORY PASSAGE

"Don't hurt him." Aiden's voice shook ever so slightly. He hoped Jesse got the hint. "See we'll put them down very gently. We wouldn't want them to go off and accidentally conk you in the wonkus."

"Go on!" Bishop hissed red-faced but now completely focused on the boys.

Aiden took a knee and waited for Logan to do the same. Then he reached out to very slowly set his hammer down and said. "Be careful Logan. We don't want to conk anyone!"

Suddenly a bright blue blur shot from their left and slammed into Bishop's temple. Mitchell took advantage of the distraction and elbowed Bishop in the stomach and tried to break free as the man staggered back.

But Bishop reacted quicker than Aiden expected, and he managed to catch Mitchell's wrist.

"Mitchell, drop!" Lauren called her spear back in her hand.

Mitchell let his legs fall out from under him, and she whipped the spear into Bishop and the man disappeared in a poof of light.

"No!" Refi'Cul screamed as thunder cracked and rain began to fall. "Kill these accursed children once and for all!"

HOW DO YOU CELEBRATE YOUR VICTORIES?

PASSAGE QUESTIONS

Read the STORY PASSAGE and answer the following questions in your reading journal.

1. How does Aiden create a diversion?
2. Why are they able to defeat Bishop?
3. How does Refi'Cul react?

DAY FIVE

READING & MEMORY VERSE

Today, read chapters forty-four and the epilogue in the book. Recite this week's memory verse aloud and complete the activity below. Include the coloring page and vocabulary puzzle with today's activities.

ACTIVITY: BOOTS OF PEACE RACE

MATERIALS

- Pair of adult big boots
- Pair of adult flip-flops or sandals
- Racer's own athletic tennis shoes
- Any objects to make an obstacle course
- Timer

INSTRUCTIONS

1. Have fun making an indoor or outdoor obstacle course. Be sure to include things to run around, hop over, etc.
2. See how fast the racer(s) can run the course wearing each pair of shoes. Start with the adult shoes and end with your own shoes.
3. Time each race.
4. When the results are in talk about how much more confident you felt running the course in your own shoes.
5. How is this like wearing the Boots of Peace?

Knowing that we have peace with God helps us to be confident. Jesus has already defeated Satan. "Ye are of God, little children, and have overcome them: because greater is he that is in you, than he that is in the world." —1 John 4:4 KJV

DISCUSS WAYS THAT GOD GIVES YOU PEACE.

ANSWER KEY

LIGHT OF MINE

WEEK ONE: SHINING LIGHT

DAY ONE

1. Father builds the tower to light the area where he works to keep him safe.
2. Frogs and ducks visit the farm.
3. Father builds defenses.
4. Not necessarily. They love money, but they don't all love the Lord.
5. The light is a reflection of the Savior's Light. It comes from God.

DAY TWO

1. Mother closes the shutters on the tower during the storm.
2. Aiden thought lightning struck the windmill because part of it melted.
3. Aiden thought the Dark One was responsible for the windmill because the Dark One likes to grumble to lessen the light.
4. Mother thinks the tower being closed up may have led to Father's disappearance.
5. Mother tells the kids they can trust the Parson.

DAY THREE

1. Lauren used a slate and check list to organize the work.
2. Ethan's special friend is Sparkle Frog.
3. Ethan was proud that he retrieved half a bucket of water and filled up the pot.
4. Lauren uses Mother's tactics to help make sure it doesn't happen again.

DAY FOUR

1. Aiden's special friend is Daddy Duck.
2. The Parson comes to visit the children.
3. The carpenters were supposed to visit the children.
4. Aiden uses a harrow to fix the windmill.
5. The stories Lauren reads from the Good Book all describe the Holy Spirit coming upon people.

SECRET MESSAGE

A cadre of mercenaries muted the music while they contemplated the ceramic cat lying in the loft.

WEEK TWO: FACING TRAILS

DAY ONE

1. The kids are excited to see the Parson, because he will give them guidance.
2. There is darkness in the direction of the church.
3. Ethan returned with Sparkle Frog.
4. The Knight Protector storms out of the church after he called the Bishop's sermon heresey.

DAY TWO

1. Sparkle Frog heals bruises and contusions.
2. The children are treated harshly and dismissed.
3. A horn is sent with the children. It's a horn that even the hounds of hell respect.
4. A writ with Father's instructions is shown to the children.
5. The Violet Acolyte returns home with the children.

DAY THREE

1. The sky is clear and bright as they travel home.
2. The acolyte questions whether the Parson has something to do with the Darkness.
3. The acolyte freaks out when he meets Daddy Duck.
4. The Tower had been boarded up in the children's absence.

DAY FOUR

1. He didn't know anything about the Light or the song "This Little Light of Mine."
2. He ate pork and potatoes for lunch, which is not proper for the Sabbath.
3. Meow Meow plays with the tassles on the bottom of the acolyte's robe.
4. The acolyte appologized for not respecting the children's conscience.

WORD SCRAMBLE

1. AREONTGGNC: Congregant
2. ACRASYNUT: Sanctuary
3. CREHTIE: Heretic
4. CNATRSEMA: Sacrament
5. LERGA: Regal
6. AIUTLR: Ritual

WEEK THREE: ARMOR OF GOD

DAY ONE

1. Meow Meow's power wakes up the children.
2. Their quest leads them to the Parson's house.
3. The children find a darkness machine.
4. Aiden's sword blazes with fire, and he uses it to destroy the locks. Then, Daddy Duck directs the Light.
5. The children see the Knight Protector.

DAY TWO

1. The children bring the acolyte berries.
2. The Dandelion Acolyte shows up with the proclamation that the kids are to leave home.
3. Locks and hinges are added to the tower.

DAY THREE

1. Lauren knocks out the acolyte when she uses her spear.
2. The Knight Protector gets away.
3. The kids find the Knight Protector. He is knocked out and looks a bit different.
4. Ethan finds a dark bag that loses things inside it.

DAY FOUR

1. Aiden suggests they lay a trap for the Knight Protector.
2. They attached a heavy bag of grain to a rope and rig it to drop on the Knight Protector.

MAZE

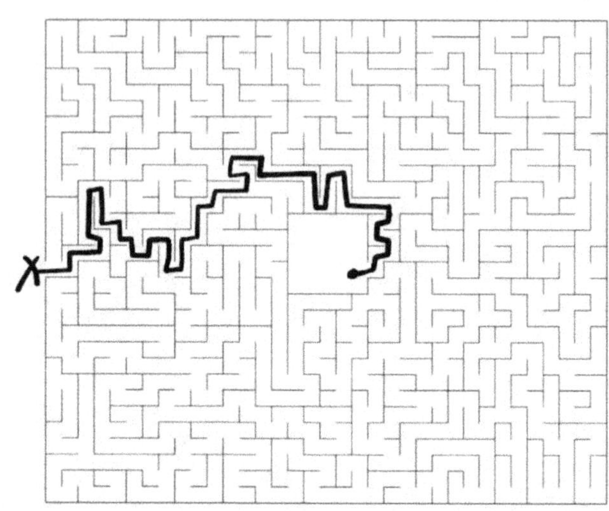

WEEK FOUR: HOLY SPIRIT

DAY ONE

1. Yes, the Knight Protector was knocked out.
2. The acolyte wants to kill the Knight Protector.
3. Ethan jumps on the knight to protect him from the acolyte.
4. The Knight Protector says he was sent to watch over the children and to find out the plot of the Darkness.
5. Hell Hounds and Yoinu Censer appear when the Acolyte blows his horn.

DAY TWO

1. He tells Ethan to let his light shine.
2. Hell Hounds attack the acolyte when he tries to help the children.
3. The Holy Spirit powers Lauren's spear to knock the Darkness out of people, Aiden's sword to cut through magical objects, and Ethan's shield to destory darkness monsters with the Light.
4. No. The censer is destroyed by the Light.
5. The Bishop runs off.

DAY THREE

1. The children prayed for him, but they didn't get the answer they hoped for. However, God's plans are higher than our own and He is always faithful.

DAY FOUR

1. Mother was in a dark room.

WORD SEARCH

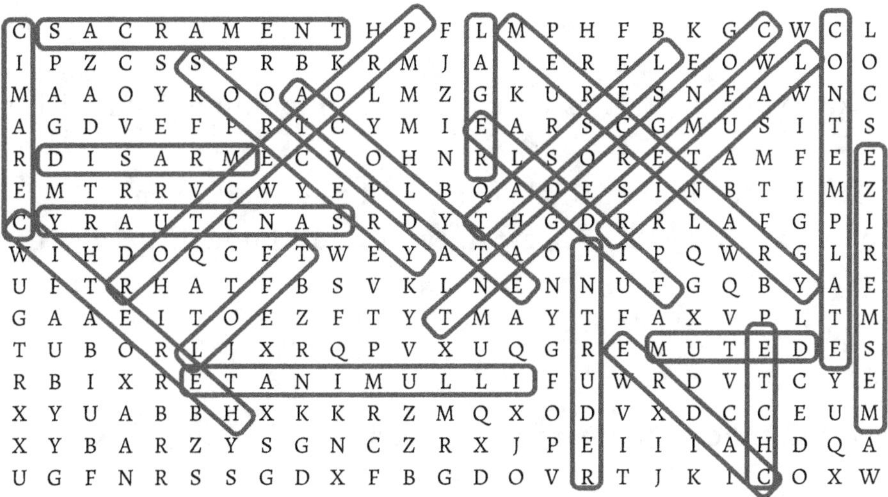

STILL SMALL VOICE

WEEK ONE: A SMALL VOICE

DAY ONE

1. He means they are keeping information to themselves and not seeking advice from others.
2. "With the deception of the bishop and even my own behavior, it has to be difficult for you to trust anyone."
3. Ethan is more concerned about eating.
4. "He had a plate of bacon and flapjacks in front of him, and his stomach was aching."

DAY TWO

1. The Knight Protector discovered a Darkness machine.
2. Aiden was angry that the Knight Protector didn't knock it down.
3. "Aiden balled his fists and put them on his hips."
4. The Knight Protector didn't knock it down because the still small voice told him to wait and see.

DAY THREE

1. The kids wanted to wait for the Knight Protector.
2. The Knight Protector went to town to make plans to travel to Blooming Glen.
3. Uncle wants the kids to go to Gran's, their grandmother.
4. Uncle believes the kids should be with family and he has written instructions that specify the kids should go to Gran's.

DAY FOUR

1. The chldren believe the small voice is urging them to go to Blooming Glen with the Knight Protector.
2. No, they have doubts and are uncertain that Uncle has heard the small voice.
3. "The quiver in Aiden's voice gave away his uncertainty. 'I don't know if he heard the small voice.'"

SECRET MESSAGE

A crescendo of lacquer encased the silhouetted pantomine during the prologue as a silent metaphor.

WEEK TWO: THE LOST

DAY ONE

1. Uncle means that family loyalty is more important than loyalty to those who aren't family.
2. Uncle is suspicious and doesn't trust the Knight Protector.
3. Uncle tells the kids they need to stick with him and puts his hands on his hips. Then, he says, "So, you need to follow my lead regardless of what kind of story the Knight Protector might be telling."

DAY TWO

1. Sir Nicolas died.
2. Ethan prayed for Sir Nicolas to get better.
3. Ethan asked Parson to pray for Sir Nicolas to be all better. Then, Ethan said he prayed but it didn't work.
4. Parson said Sir Nicolas was in heaven, that his mission was complete, and he was free from pain and conflict

DAY THREE

1. Uncle wouldn't listen to her.
2. Lauren took a moment to realize that it wouldn't help to insist Uncle listen to her.
3. Because they aren't following the still small voice.
4. Lauren hopes her grandmother, who follows the Light, will help them.

DAY FOUR

1. Daddy Duck tried to fly away.
2. Aiden wobbled and had to grab the wagon's rail to keep from falling off.
3. Ethan laughed.
4. Aiden.
5. Aiden didn't want to admit defeat.

WORD SCRAMBLE

1. ATENOR: Ornate
2. ALETML: Mallet
3. ONUISN: Unison
4. UNOPEC: Pounce
5. ALTNO: Talon
6. ARADM: Drama

WEEK THREE: IN THE BELLY

DAY ONE

1. Uncle was embarrased, but pleased by the display of affection.
2. Uncle squirmed, looked panicked, and then patted Ethan on the head.
3. Lauren was angry about Uncle teaching methods.
4. "Lauren was not all that hppy with Uncle's teaching methods. He could have helped Aiden with the duck the day before to keep him safe."
5. Lauren was grateful Uncle let her bring her cat, Meow Meow.

DAY TWO

1. Uncle is angry the children joined the fight.
2. He wanted them to hide.
3. Uncle killed the cougar.
4. Lauren knocked it out first.
5. Uncle isn't a believer. He doesn't follow the Light.

DAY THREE

1. Heath Wardens are giants.
2. The acolyte believes the censors bring the one true light.
3. He follows the Darkness, but doesn't know it.
4. Yes.
5. The mother and daughter sat at table. The acolyte stood nearby and when the mother notices him, she tells him to start getting ready for the lunch rush.

DAY FOUR

1. Because Sparkle Frog healed him.
2. "Sparkle Frog makes head eggs go away."
3. She believes the girl's attack may have been prevented if more men sought the Light.
4. The matron is referring to the girl.

MAZE

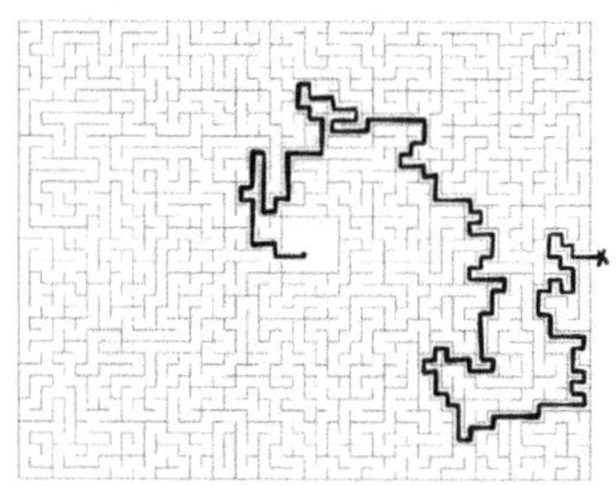

WEEK FOUR: HOLY SPIRIT

DAY ONE

1. They are in a barn.
2. Tok.
3. Tok asks the kids to help him save his bear.
4. The kids are uncertain about helping because their Uncle wouldn't even let them scout. He wanted the to stay where they were.
5. Tok's eyes fill with tears.

DAY TWO

1. The kids left the stable after he told them not to.
2. Worried.
3. Lauren thinks, *"No! Ethan, why'd you open your mouth?"* She also attempts to diffuse the situation.

DAY THREE

1. They are fighting a giant.
2. The iron contraption on the giant's back is spewing black smoke into the air.
3. Uncle is now a believer, and the Light is guiding him into battle.

DAY FOUR

1. The frontiersman was floating on the Awoi River.
2. It was around dawn when he was pulled ashore.
3. The geese carried him to shore.
4. It was around noon when he finally opened his eyes.

WORD SEARCH

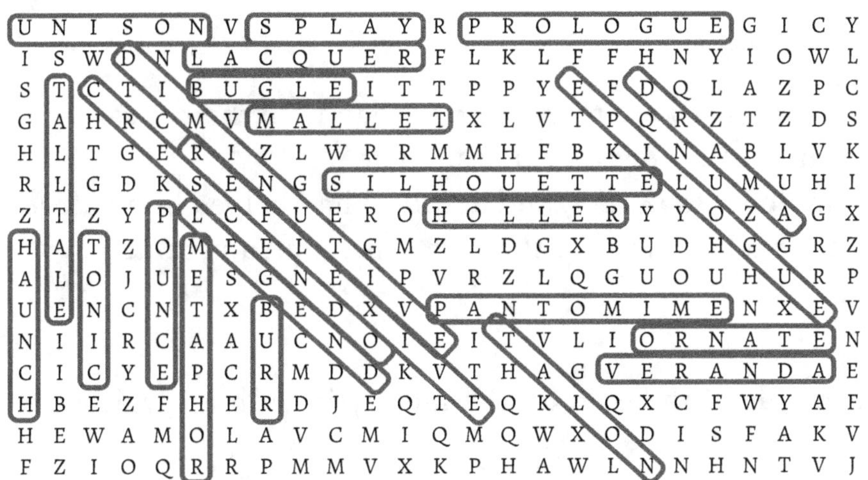

FEAR NO EVIL

WEEK ONE: SEPARATED

DAY ONE

1. The Lord is our shepherd because he cares for us, protects us, and laid His life down to save us. We should learn to know his voice and follow Him.
2. No, his heart didn't actually move. It means that he felt suddenly frightened.
3. Uncle is trying to reassure the children to have faith that God would protect them. He is reminding them that God delivered them there, where there were many people that were willing to fight for the children.

DAY TWO

1. It means that Lauren lost her courage for a moment. She was too scared to do what was asked of her.
2. It says she was "blankly staring," "she was drained," and "her limbs were frozen."
3. She is scared because Aiden was knocked in the water. She is scared of the carp knocking her into the water too.

DAY THREE

1. She thinks that Tye is calling her a liar.
2. She believed Lauren because she said that she saw the Arcoirisana bless her.
3. Abomination means something that causes hatred or a feeling of disgust or loathing. Tye cannot imagine another warden using evil against creatures that they have always been sworn to protect.
4. She asks Tye to help her find her brothers.

DAY FOUR

1. Menacing means to threaten. So, they were threatening Ethan with their spears.
2. He felt afraid. He realized that the Darkness was in that place.
3. Ethan thought about what the Good Book said, and how God had helped him before.
4. He thought he could distract them by talking to them and then outrun them.

SECRET MESSAGE

An abomination of rites! Banished, he clambered up the mountain with a spyglass and a rudder.

WEEK TWO: ALLIANCES

DAY ONE

1. She means that the bear doesn't really understand what it is doing because it is corrupted by the Darkness.
2. Lauren remembers that after she knocked the Darkness out of Tok's bear with her spear, it became kind again.
3. Feeling overwhelmed by something causes many strong emotions all at once that are often stressful, and it feels like you cannot overcome the situation.
4. Lauren feels overwhelmed because she knows that trying to explain salvation to Tye is very important. She wants to do it right, and she thinks that she has to explain the whole Good Book.

DAY TWO

1. The food has been cooked over the censer, therefore it has been corrupted by the Darkness.
2. Ethan tries saying things like "No, thank you," and "My Daddy wouldn't like that." He tells Chief he has his own food. When Chief calls his food "Ba'bee food," Ethan replies, "Well, I guess I'm a baby then."
3. Chief has already been corrupted by the Darkness. In his mind, he thinks that if Ethan eats the food, he will become strong like him.

DAY THREE

1. She felt guilty because she was scared of the carp and hid when they were attacked on the ferry. Without her help, Aiden and Knight Protector were stung by the carp.
2. Tye's brother was taken by a mother bear. Tye was supposed to be watching him but left him sleeping while she went for a swim in the creek.
3. Lauren told Tye about what is says in the Good Book. Lauren tells her it says, "…if we believe in the Savior and confess our misdeeds, we will be forgiven."

DAY FOUR

1. It won't work because everyone would see him crush the globe into the water. He needed to crush the globe into the actual pool of water for nobody to see him do it.
2. He uses words like "by my own hands." He says that "it will be by my own hands that I take the waters of my destiny." He claims that he is being too superior by standing over the people while the water makes its choice. By pretending to be timid and respectful, Refi'Cul is getting the high priestess to give him his way.
3. A penitent man is someone who is humble or repentant.

WEEK TWO: ALLIANCES

WORD SCRAMBLE

1. DRAECHR: Charred
2. NAIGGOFR: Foraging
3. ARERDGNU: Grandeur
4. ETFAELRD: Faltered
5. CKLASMREHA: Ramshackle
6. VNNEGACEE: Vengeance

WEEK THREE: TRAPPED

DAY ONE

1. Ethan said that it was because he "shared his food with him."
2. Besta implied that before Darkness they shared food with bears too.
3. Besta was sad because the Darkness had corrupted the bears and her people.
4. All of the things that Besta told him made Ethan realize how much they needed the Light to protect them.

DAY TWO

1. He prayed and asked God for help.
2. When he told Mama what he thought they should do, his sword erupted into flame.
3. She agreed by nodding, but she was still sad to leave Father.

DAY THREE

1. Ethan found a dagger in the box. He thought it would help him free Baby Bear.
2. Answers will vary, but consider how God sometimes puts things in just the right places at just the right times.
3. Lok's people naturally take care of the bears. However, it was also used as a strategy to help slow Mama bear down.

DAY FOUR

1. Tye threw Lauren's spear at the bear and hit it in the chest.
2. Tye thought Lauren saved her brother because she brought him out of the cave. She did not yet realize that she had the power of God's Light.
3. "She laughed as tears of joy ran down her face."

MAZE

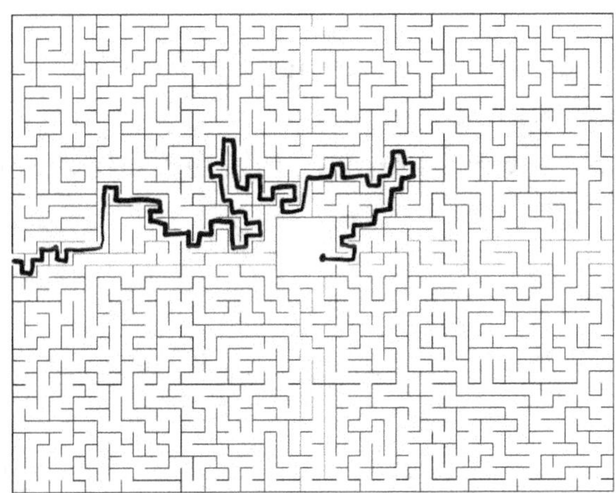

WEEK FOUR: RESCUED

DAY ONE

1. Chief believed if the bear ate Ethan that they could eat the bear and get strong.
2. His "heart leapt" and "tears burst from his eyes."
3. The other Bjorn-born with Chief came out with their spears, but they seemed to "falter" when they heard Lok say that what they were doing was not their "way."
4. Ethan thought Tye was powerful because of her size, and how Chief was "catapulted"when she hit him with Lauren's spear.

DAY TWO

1. She knew what would happen to the door if he cut through it in that spot.
2. Aiden didn't listen because he was hurt and was being impatient.
3. The door slammed and tipped inward towards them. Mother dove and tackled Aiden out of the way. The door crashed to the floor loudly, alerting the enemy to their escape route.

DAY THREE

1. Lauren told him there was food in her pouch. Knowing he was in a hurry, she asked him if he wanted to sit down and have a "full lunch."
2. She didn't want him looking in the pouch because the dagger was in it.
3. If Skull Crusher would have agreed to a "full lunch" it would have slowed them down more, giving Tye a chance to catch up to them.
4. Her backup plan was to use the dagger to cut them free from the net.

DAY FOUR

1. They are trying to get away from Refi'Cul and the Steele Brothers.
2. They have just defeated Skull Crusher in a battle. He has been hit with Lauren's spear and is unconscious.
3. Knight Protector is going to take all of the horses and lead them off in a different direction than the family, in hopes that the enemy follows him.
4. If they can get to Blooming Glen and light the tower there, then everything and everyone hit by its Light will be protected from the Darkness.

WEEK FOUR: RESCUED

WORD SEARCH

```
Q K M L F A C E T S L I W G Y M W C V Q U Z V M P
A Q E M F E B K M U U D L N Z A R R L K B H Q A N
X V F J J Y I O D T R W M H P J D R R U D D E R Y
O S R G R J T J M L U A I A N G U I S H R K A D K
S V Q F R F T F E I V N M O R Q R T E C C Q R D D
I L E Z C A F W A H N E I S C X V E V Z G P H N O
N B P R S L N O H L D A N C H A P O T H E C A R Y
F A E C S P A D R L T M T G Y A G X L E A N T O D
I N N T P H Y M E A K E M I E J C C O N S O L E D
R I D P X A A G B U G J R I O A M K C H A R R E D
M S U F T K T D L E R I L E U N N T L H I L T C M
A H L P H Z T N O A R K N A D O Y C G E Z X D Z K
R E U X P U Z W A W S E N G I V U B E X J S K Z S
Y D M M B Z J T K K E S D A I J O F J J N I K S G
S T A L A C T I T E S D E S A A K O M I N O U S W
```

ARMOR OF GOD

WEEK ONE: FACING TRIALS

DAY ONE

1. Answers will vary.
2. Having a "stern visage" means that Mother had a serious expression. So, to say it cracked means she stopped having that expression at once.
3. Mother is upset because she is very worried about Father. She wants to help him as soon as possible.

DAY TWO

1. This actually doesn't mean that he clicked his tongue. It's a gesture using suction to make a sound with the tongue against the back of the teeth, and is typically used to express disapproval or impatience.
2. Tye's father silences her. He doesn't allow her to tell her side of the story.
3. PART 1; Answers will vary. Skull Crusher may have used the grief and disappointment that they already had for the situation involving Tye. Darkness may have been at work here as well and be affecting the giants' decisions. PART 2: This answer is found in the text before this reading passage. The children saw the plants had been affected by the darkness and that the sky was also much darker. They described it as a "double-darkness zone".

DAY THREE

1. Running at full tilt means running at top speed or as fast as you can.
2. It is harmed because Skull Crusher has already made them believe that the humans have attacked him. The giants already believe humans are bad, so the humans being at the village only makes Skull Crushers' story seem more valid.
3. Answers will vary.

DAY FOUR

1. Answers will vary.
2. The text states "That axe meant the difference between life and death in the wilderness. Without it, he couldn't build shelter, make fire, or defend himself. Plus, it was. . . special. . . his brother had given it to him."
3. Answers will vary. His hands were burned when he picked up the axe.

WEEK ONE: FACING TRIALS

SECRET MESSAGE

A din outside pierced the stern visage of my boon companion as he moved the pommel on the oxidized, tempered sword.

WEEK TWO: SEEKING TRUTH

DAY ONE

1. Answers will vary. "Disabuse you of that notion" means to free someone of a belief. So, in this case, Prime Sister meant to change Ethan's beliefs, which she believed to be wrong.
2. He is trying to run the cord over the sharp thorn in hopes that it will cut it so he can get free.
3. Answers will vary.

DAY TWO

1. Answers will vary. Ethan cried when his shield was put in the censer
2. Answers will vary. His words were, "You're in big trouble now! My Mama's gonnaget you!"
3. Answers will vary.

DAY THREE

1. The cord got caught on the log as it was swept down the river. Chief does not want the log to drag all of the Bjorn Born down the river with it. By cutting the cord they are all tied to, he hopes to save the ones that are already on the other side of the river and give the others a chance to swim to safety.
2. Answers will vary.
3. Answers will vary.

DAY FOUR

1. Answers will vary.
2. Answers will vary.
3. Answers will vary.

WORD SCRAMBLE

1. SOUCARU: Raucous
2. TRFUASQREAFT: Quarterstaff
3. RACMIEGD: Grimaced
4. NSLAAER: Arsenal
5. TRHIGEBL: Blight
6. SIOONXU: Noxious

WEEK THREE: SHARING FAITH

DAY ONE

1. Answers will vary.
2. Father got the idea from the verse ing the Good Book about the whole armor of God.
3. Answers will vary.

DAY TWO

1. Tye's bump did not go away.
2. Answers will vary.
3. Answers will vary.

DAY THREE

1. Tok is angry at his father because he feels like he let the Darkness into the village and that he should have agreed to help.
2. He is sad that Ethan is lost and wants to help save him.
3. Mother helps Tok understand that his father changed, and his feelings are not good enough reasons to disobey his father.

DAY FOUR

1. Refi'Cul thinks having Ethan tell the story will make Ethan and his family look bad. Instead, Ethan tells the truth and brings to light all of the Steele Brothers' and Refi'Cul's mistakes.
2. Since the Steele Brothers did not correctly corrupt the armor, it is now a weakness. Champion says, "If I gently tap one of those fools with this sword while they're wearing that armor, they'll turn to rust."
3. Ethan had already told many things that had caused Father to become angry with Refi'Cul. Then, when Father asked Ethan what happened to the censer, Ethan smiled as he responded.

MAZE

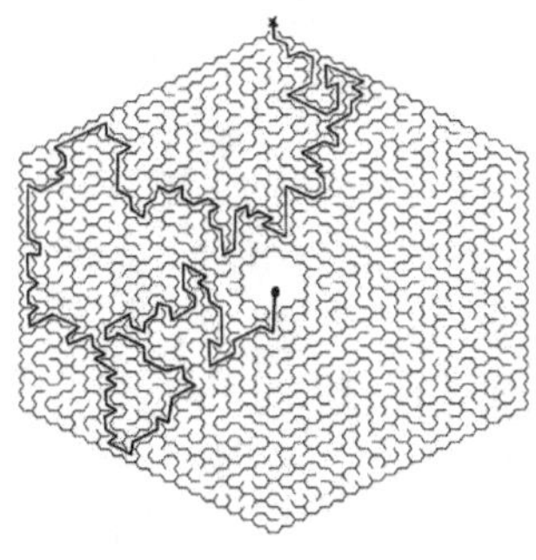

WEEK FOUR: PERSEVERING

DAY ONE

1. Tye refused to ride in the wagon and ran next to the horses.
2. Tye only rides in the wagon when ordered to by Mother. Tye will not speak to Lauren even when Lauren speaks to her. She will not acknowledge her at all, even when Lauren puts her arm around her.
3. Answers will vary.

DAY TWO

1. Ethan was surprised when Lauren and Aiden stood up in the wagon and joined him in singing.
2. Ethan caught Father in the wheelbarrow as he fell, and he ran with him to the lake.
3. Answers will vary. Father was not wearing armor that was not fully corrupted. Also, Father was not fully corrupted by the Darkness.

DAY THREE

1. They tap the corrupted weapons and armor with their Holy weapons.
2. She asks Mother about it because of the snow globe that she found.
3. Mother says that hopefully, Father will be able to drink the water from the Wellspring of Life.

DAY FOUR

1. Answers will vary.
2. Answers will vary.
3. Answers will vary.

WEEK FOUR: PERSEVERING

WORD SEARCH

R C O N C U S S I V E W I N C E D E U P Z P T L A
S C P Y I H L C O C Y F R A C A S Z P O G D I N R
T K O N K Q S A T K T D L S K D Y Q H M N K P N S
L E G Y W I P C B L I G H T E R K J C M M O J W E
F K U W P B X H G Q V I A N D U J U K E O J M N
G E Y S E R V E R F U B Q Y U G H F N L F E R A
Q H W O B S G H B O O N C O M P A N I O N F E L
Z W R X J H A P M D E D S Y K V I S A G E U X I D
T G A I E A R R I M Q U A R T E R S T A F F C O E
P G U D I C R I A W P X A J U B G A X I V U S S
A Y C S G K I Z E Q J A B S O L V E K L D X U H
L U O I W L S E R E A P F D K S G L W U U S R O
L Q U G E E O I E Y D L H P D P A S S E L L S D
L I S D E N I R K Z J C S P R E Z H T B M Z S D
T E M P E R I N G U B Z K K P H T Q R P O S M Y Y

WELLSPRING OF LIFE

WEEK ONE: NEW STRATEGIES

DAY ONE

1. Ethan would not take Sarah's lantern. He told her that she would need it to protect her family. He promised her that he would come back with help.
2. In the passage, it said "his heart swelled in his chest." Knowing there were more Light Bearers fighting the Darkness gave Ethan confidence.
3. Sarah offered Ethan her lantern. She also told Ethan that even though there was Darkness, her parents stayed because they felt it was their mission.

DAY TWO

1. Mother explains the real deceiver is the Bishop.
2. Ethan wants Iron Sister to stay. He refers to her as "my Iron Sister." Answers will vary to the second half of the question.

DAY THREE

1. Aiden worried his map was wrong, and that Tye would end up going in the wrong direction. Lauren suggested they try to find horses so Tye wouldn't have to journey alone.
2. In the passage, the phrase means he emphasized the urgency to encourage action.
3. Tye going alone is a risk because there would be no one to help her if she needed it. Also, Tye is still not acting like herself, and they don't understand why.

DAY FOUR

1. Gramps knew there was water in the grove because he said, "Trees don't grow up in the prairie without lots of fresh water."
2. It means Ethan was experiencing feelings of great happiness or joy.
3. Answers will vary.

SECRET MESSAGE

Pronto! A cacophony of irony will befall the exasperated hero before a moment of respite.

WEEK TWO: FRIEND OR FOE

DAY ONE

1. Answers will vary.
2. If someone acts treacherously, they betray someone.
3. Tye interrupts Lauren. She states, "Enough of your explanations."

DAY TWO

1. In the passage, "Ethan's jaw set hard" meant he was experiencing strong emotions about losing the snow globe, and he was trying to hold back his feelings.
2. Jesse is frustrated, and Ethan is mad at himself.
3. Gramps finds prints in the dust and concludes the prairie dogs took the snow globe.

DAY THREE

1. Aiden felt responsible for getting the wagon repaired quickly, especially since he didn't know what happened to the rest of his family.
2. Mother sensed that Aiden was feeling insecure about his abilities.
3. Answers will vary.

DAY FOUR

1. Logan offered his hatchet to Aiden to keep when he saw how well it worked with Aiden's hammer.
2. This means that they are better together. They need each other to help one another.
3. Answers will vary.

WORD SCRAMBLE

1. LESIUEV: Elusive
2. UDAPTUTCNE: Punctuated
3. EROMEBMCSU: Cumbersome
4. INOLBA: Albino
5. ERODURFW: Furrowed
6. VEIGRASNL: Slavering

WEEK THREE: CROSSFIRE

DAY ONE

1. Ethan fears Mother will not be able to find them if they go off of the path.
2. Jesse's plan was cut arrows into the ground with his sword to mark the path.
3. Uncle is afraid using the sword will start a fire.

DAY TWO

1. If they don't regulate their speed, they will be exhausted and unable to fight whoever they catch up to.
2. They hope there will be others at the settlement to help fight whoever is carrying the Censer.
3. Answers will vary.

DAY THREE

1. Ethan thinks it is the Wellspring of Life because it was on the snow globe, and there is a beautiful fountain there.
2. Krystal is trying to relate to them in a way they will understand. She wants to be sure that they place value on understanding what she has to tell them.
3. Answers will vary.

DAY FOUR

1. Ethan says this because Aiden ambushed Skull Crusher in the wagon. Also, Sparkle Frog has just leaped out of the wagon toward Tye.
2. Lauren thinks Skull Crusher is now outnumbered, and they will be able to defeat him.
3. Answers will vary.

MAZE

WEEK FOUR: WELLSPRING OF LIFE

DAY ONE

1. Darkness had corrupted the plant.
2. Dumbfounded means to be amazed or greatly astonished.
3. Answers will vary. Tye is in shock by the events that have taken place, and she is having trouble reacting in the moment.

DAY TWO

1. Tye planned to execute Skull Crusher.
2. Tye believes it is her right to decide Skull Crusher's fate since he hurt her father and wronged her as well.
3. Mother helped Tye understand that Skull Crusher needed to answer for what he had done in front of all her people so that her name would be cleared.

DAY THREE

1. Answers will vary.
2. He told them about Refi'Cul's plans at Blooming Glen.
3. Answers will vary.

DAY FOUR

1. Journey Leader doesn't understand why Refi'Cul is making such a spectacle. He thinks he is making the task of destroying the tower too difficult.
2. Refi'Cul thinks he is setting an example for the people by having the Light Bearers tear down the tower.
3. It means that someone has been acting foolishly.

WORD SEARCH

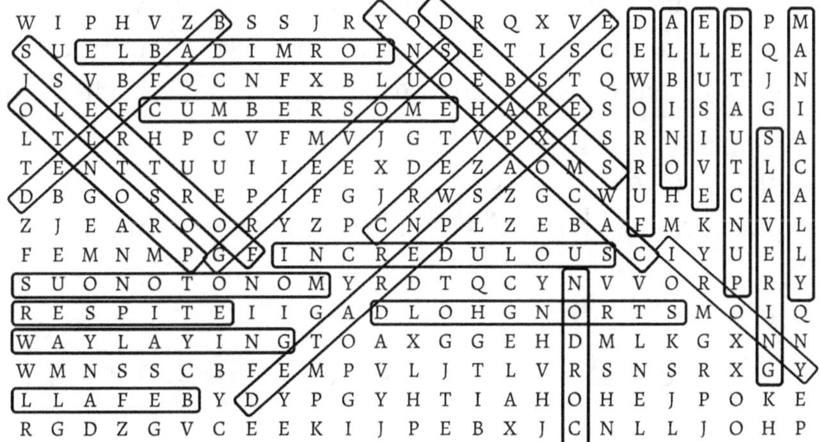

DEMOLISHING THE STRONGHOLD

WEEK ONE: DARKNESS

DAY ONE

1. If Journey Leader was loyal to Tye, then he would protect her and her friends. This would give them more allies and cause more problems for Refi'Cul.
2. Refi'Cul was suggesting that Skull Crusher kill Journey Leader, make it look like an accident, and that he would not be given any consequences for it.
3. Answers will vary.

DAY TWO

1. Mother is overcome with emotions when her eyes meet Lauren's. She is proud of her daughter's courage but is worried about the danger that is still ahead. It causes a tear in her eye.
2. To scrutinize something means to analyze or examine something very closely.
3. Answers will vary.

DAY THREE

1. Since the ram's horn was of the Darkness, it was sucking in the light around it making it look like the Darkness was eating up the light.
2. Mother saw Skull Crusher.
3. It means that any resistance or attempt to fight back will be unsuccessful.

DAY FOUR

1. The smoke from the dragon made Tye's skin feel like it had been "whipped with stinging nettles." The smoke slowed her movements like she was stuck in cobwebs. The smoke also filled up the area so that Tye couldn't see anything. It made it seem like she was in an "abyss." All of these things caused a sense of hopelessness in Tye. The text says it "caused despair to creep in."
2. The Armor of God protected Tye's head from the fumes.
3. Tye's sword blade began to glow again and her hand that held it no longer stung.

SECRET MESSAGE

Glyphs on the battlement guided the malcontent, vendetta-seeking garrison towards calamity.

WEEK TWO: FAITH

DAY ONE

1. Master Warden knows as more time passes the Darkness affects their lands more.
2. Father says they need a weapon to defeat the dragon.
3. This phrase comes from the Bible. Psalm 8:2 states: "Out of the mouth of babes and infants, you have established strength because of your foes, to still the enemy and the avenger." This means that God can even use children to accomplish great things and children sometimes have honesty and unexpected wisdom to offer.

DAY TWO

1. Bishop was sending Mercenary Captain and Master at Arms with a militia to attack the children in the Grove of Righteousness. They were to carry packs of Y'lohnu globes to corrupt the bears and cougars that lived in the caves and trees along the way.
2. Bishop planned the meeting in the jail so that Mother would be able to hear the plans about her family being attacked.
3. Mother did not show any weakness to Bishop. Instead, she created doubt with her confidence. She told him that his troops were destined to be defeated if they went to the grove and that his "false light" had not told him anything.

DAY THREE

1. Her plan is for Daddy Duck to shine his Light on the foundry's smokestack so that the other birds will follow it.
2. Answers will vary.
3. Answers will vary.

DAY FOUR

1. The text says "Not having Master Warden's disapproving stare boring into him helped him relax and do the job."
2. Answers will vary.

WORD SCRAMBLE

1. ALARPY: Parlay
2. LEFRANCLTES: crestfallen
3. ATTRALECION: Altercation
4. OSGINT: Ingots
5. SINNEZED: Denizens
6. ISOFBUR: Fibrous

WEEK THREE: CALL TO ARMS

DAY ONE

1. The text says, "Ethan's heart leapt in his chest," which means that he was overcome with joy.
2. Originally Ethan smiles because he agrees with the statement, but then he realizes that if it is Knight Protector's son and he has turned to the Darkness, then that will hurt Knight Protector.
3. It is Knight Protector.

DAY TWO

1. Answers will vary.
2. Answers will vary.
3. Answers will vary.

DAY THREE

1. Answers will vary.
2. The Steele Brother's other routes of escape were blocked off by the Light. They also may have thought the fire and smoke would give them strength and camouflage.
3. A bucket brigade is a line of people who pass buckets of water from person to person to put out a fire.

DAY FOUR

1. Lauren is trying to protect Mitchell from the dragon's blasts of smoke.
2. The force of the dragon's blast knocks them all down, but the armor of God glows and protects them from the harm of the smoke.
3. It makes him think about how the giants must have felt when they were blasted by the Light.

MAZE

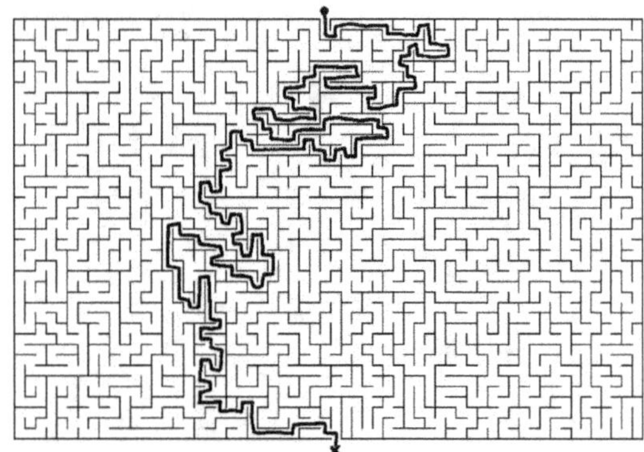

WEEK FOUR: LIGHT

DAY ONE

1. Mother smiles at Tye with kindness and puts her hands together and her head down in prayer.
2. Tye follows Mother's lead and prays.
3. Answers will vary.

DAY TWO

1. Lauren was afraid that she wouldn't be able to hit the dragon because she wouldn't be able to see it at night.
2. The jewel in her spear glittered. It reminded Lauren that if God was for her then what could stand against her?
3. They were using the dragon to attack them with its smoke.

DAY THREE

1. The Calamitous Drake "disappears in a shower of white sparks" after Lauren hits it with her spear.
2. Bishop takes Mitchell as a hostage.
3. Answers will vary.

DAY FOUR

1. Aiden makes a point of saying to Bishop that they are carefully putting their weapons down so that they don't accidentally conk him in the wonkus, giving Jesse a hint of what they need him to do.
2. They are able to defeat Bishop because they work as a team and listen to each other well.
3. Refi'Cul shouts "No!" and orders the Steele Brothers to kill the children. He rushes towards them with his dagger.

WEEK FOUR: LIGHT

WORD SEARCH

```
D X T C I N G O T S A G J L C I R Z M K W N M R X
P R O F F E R I N G Y U X M P D R W F Y Z B V N V P
A S G F E L Q C M C G H C B A G E E V J G Z N O E A
N G T E E E D X R S A E P O A L A N M P N G N O N R
H P F L M R A I A E V L O D M T C R I B M J Q D L
F H A I J B O J S O S N A H I P T O R Z L G O T A Y
F S C R N I O C D G P T X M X M A L N I E E S T T K
I T K A L O L I U P T F M I H P T E T S N M B A S
B C A Q G P A W D T Q L F A I T D E R M E O S R U F
R A K H L U E K U E Y K O X L F Y J N I E N N B S T
O T J Y A D T D K N O I C Q L F C S D O N T U Z V
U I F P L D X V Y E L W D W E D S K I T T S R Z X
S C H S F N M T L H D M S Q G N E S I N S U L
M A G F V N G E M A L T E R C A T I O N G P X
Q D U L I M E L E E C G T V X I Z B A N T E R R L
```